Anderson Public Library
114 N. Main
Lawrenceburg, KY 40342

THAT AWKWARD
AGE

Book Two of the Last Fool Series

BILL MYERS

D1559469

That Awkward Age
The Last Fool Series – Book Two
© Copyright 2014 Bill Myers

Published by:
Amaris Media International
www.Amarismedia.com

Cover © Jun Ares

"All rights reserved by author. No part of this publication
may be reproduced, stored in a retrieval system, or
transmitted, in any form or by any means, electronic,
mechanical, photocopying, recording, or otherwise,
without the written prior permission of the author."

"Scripture quotations marked "KJV" are taken from the
Holy Bible, King James Version, Cambridge, 1769.
Scripture taken from the New King James Version®.
Copyright © 1982 by Thomas Nelson, Inc. Used by
permission. All rights reserved.

Scripture quotations marked "NIV" are taken from HOLY
BIBLE, NEW INTERNATIONAL VERSION.
Copyright © 1973, 1978, 1984 by International Bible
Society. Used by permission of Zondervan Publishing
House."

ISBN-13 : 978-0692457566
ISBN-10: 0692457569

Praise for "Child's Play"
The Last Fool series - Book One

"Mr. Myers, have you lost your mind!"
Marty Guise, Radio host, Lay Renewal Ministries

"A great story, a funny read, with deep stuff cleverly
woven into the fabric."
Doc Kirby WTBF Radio

"Had a swell time chewing and tearing it to shreds."
Chaucer, my daughter's dog

PREVIOUS PRAISE FOR BILL MYERS

Blood of Heaven
"With the chill of a Robin Cooke techno-thriller and the
spiritual depth of a C.S. Lewis allegory, this book is a fast-paced,
action packed thriller."
—*Angela Hunt, NY Times bestselling author*

"Enjoyable and provocative. I wish I'd thought of it!"
—*Frank E. Peretti, This Present Darkness*

ELI
"The always surprising Myers has written another clever and
provocative tale."
—*Booklist*

"With this thrilling and ominous tale Myers continues to shine
brightly in speculative fiction based upon Biblical truth. Highly
recommended."
—*Library Journal*

"Myers weaves a deft, affecting tale."
—*Publishers Weekly*

The Face of God

"Strong writing, edgy...replete with action..."
—*Publishers Weekly*

Fire of Heaven
"I couldn't put the Fire of Heaven down. Bill Myers's writing is crisp, fast-paced, provocative...A very compelling story."
—*Francine Rivers, NY Times bestselling author*

Soul Tracker
"Soul Tracker provides a treat for previous fans of the author, but also a fitting introduction to those unfamiliar with his work. I'd recommend the book to anyone, initiated or not. But be careful to check your expectations at the door...it's not what you think it is."
—*Brian Reaves, Fuse magazine*

"Thought provoking and touching, this imaginative tale blends elements of science fiction with Christian theology."
—*Library Journal*

"Myers strikes deep into the heart of eternal truth with this imaginative first book of the Soul Tracker series. Readers will be eager for more."
—*Romantic Times Magazine*

Angel of Wrath
"Bill Myers is a genius.
—*Lee Stanley, producer, Gridiron Gang*

The God Hater
"When one of the most creative minds I know gets the best idea he's ever had and turns it into a novel, it's fasten-your-seat-belt time. This one will be talked about for a long time."
—*Jerry B. Jenkins author of Left Behind*

"An original masterpiece."
—*Dr. Kevin Leman, bestselling author*

"If you enjoy white-knuckle, page-turning suspense, with a brilliant blend of cutting-edge apologetics, The God Hater will grab you for a long, long time."

—*Beverly Lewis, NY Times bestselling author*

"I've never seen a more powerful and timely illustration of the incarnation. Bill Myers has a way of making the Gospel accessible and relevant to readers of all ages. I highly recommend this book."
—*Terri Blackstock, NY Times bestselling author*

"A brilliant novel that feeds the mind and heart, The God Hater belongs at the top of your reading list."
—*Angela Hunt, NY Times bestselling author*

"The God Hater is a rare combination that is both entertaining and spiritually provocative. It has a message of deep spiritual significance that is highly relevant for these times."
—*Paul Cedar, Chairman Mission America Coalition*

"Once again Myers takes us into imaginative and intriguing depths, making us feel, think and ponder all at the same time. Relevant and entertaining. The God Hater is not to be missed.
—*James Scott Bell, bestselling author*

The Voice
"A crisp, express-train read featuring 3D characters, cinematic settings and action, and, as usual, a premise I wish I'd thought of. Succeeds splendidly! Two thumbs up!"
—*Frank E. Peretti, This Present Darkness*

"Nonstop action and a brilliantly crafted young heroine will keep readers engaged as this adventure spins to its thought-provoking conclusion. This book explores the intriguing concept of God's power as not only the creator of the universe, but as its very essence."
—*Kris Wilson, CBA Magazine*

"It's a real 'what if?' book with plenty of thrills…that will definitely create questions all the way to its thought-provoking finale. The success of Myers's stories is a sweet combination of a believable storyline, intense action, and brilliantly crafted, yet flawed characters."
—*Dale Lewis, TitleTrakk.com*

The Seeing
"Compels the reader to burn through the pages. Cliff-hangers
abound and the stakes are raised higher and higher as the story
progresses—intense, action-shocking twists!"
—*TitleTrakk.com*

When the Last Leaf Falls
"A wonderful novella. Any parent will warm to the humorous
reminiscences and the loving exasperation of this father for his
strong-willed daughter...Compelling characters and fresh, vibrant
anecdotes of one family's faith journey."
—*Publishers Weekly*

Imager Chronicles
Myers is our 21st Century C.S. Lewis.
—*Light of Life Magizine*

"We . . . are being transformed into His likeness
with ever-increasing glory,
which comes from the Lord who is the Spirit."
The Apostle Paul

CHAPTER ONE

B
E
R
N
A
R
D

Hi, it's me again. Bernie? From the last book?

Maybe you know me better from all those newscasts they've been showing where I'm part of a criminal gang of mental patients who escaped and burned down the hospital a few nights ago. I don't want to be argumentative or anything, I mean if it's on the news it's got to be true, but we're really not. Criminals, I mean. Although I do feel kinda bad about the hospital part.

And I feel real bad about Trashman. We all do. Max says it was necessary for him to stay in the building to destroy our records. But it doesn't make sense to me. Then again, without my medication, what does?

In the good ol' days, (almost seventy-two hours ago), I could count on my electric razor or Darcy's dragon tattoo to help explain stuff. But now nobody's talking. Well, nobody but people and, of course, all those patterns.

I still see them, the patterns I mean. I can't paint them like I did back in my room which, like I said, kinda burned down. But I still see them. Everywhere. Like those cars down there on the freeway. See that big semi coming towards us in the left lane? And the two little compacts in the lane beside it, one near its front and the other near its back? And the blue mini-van in the next lane over, between them? See how they make the perfect letter, "**D**?"

I've been wedged under this overpass making up words all morning. Actually, it's only been one word so far. That's because it keeps showing up over and over again, which is pretty coincidental which, for me, is pretty normal. Anyways, the view up here is terrific. Saffron and JJ, the homeless couple that took us in, their camp is just on the other side of that giant, cement bulkhead. It's a great place, out of sight from the freeway traffic which is good since we're sort of celebrities now, with our faces on the news and everyone trying to arrest us. So we really appreciate them letting us stay.

JJ got real nice about it last night when we were gathered around the little fire on our plastic milk crates and wooden fruit boxes – except for Saffron who rocked back and forth in the rocker she borrowed from a local furniture store who'd left their back door unlocked. She'd really fixed up the place and even had wall-to-wall carpeting here and there from carpet samples some floor store threw away. She also had a knack for landscaping – particularly with that nice, little Christmas tree bush a few yards down from camp. How anything could grow in the cement and packed dirt is beyond me, but there it was, four feet tall and almost as round, with Christmas tree lights that didn't work and beautiful silver and gold garland. Lots and lots of garland. But I digress, which you may remember from the last book, I do a lot of.

"Ain't no deal you stayin' with us," JJ said. He threw his arm around Max and offered him a drink of his fortified wine. "Hospitalessness, it's 'cactly like homelessness . . . 'cept for a few letters here an' there."

Max nodded with that smile of his but politely refused the bottle.

No one's sure why JJ suddenly got so friendly. Joey thinks it has something to do with his romantic interests in Darcy. Ralphy thinks it's more to do with the napkins JJ stole from McDonalds. The ones he's having us autograph so he can sell them on the street. Besides his fortified wine, JJ likes his money.

And Saffron? She doesn't mind us staying either, just as long as we do our share of dumpster diving for food and keep the camp nice and tidy. And we do, well except for Winona who's always throwing up. As a health nut she doesn't do well surrounded by flesh eating bacteria and your everyday infectious diseases. She's also not fond of the smell of stale urine. Luckily, the exhaust fumes usually cover that up.

So, all in all, we're doing really good . . . except for being on the run from the police and everyone saying we're crazy. Of course Max keeps saying we're not and I wish it was true, but it's kind of hard believing him when--

Ralphy still thinks he's a superhero (and wears the goggles, shower cap and bath towel cape to prove it).

Winona is still sure she's an alien visiting from another planet (where they don't have flesh eating bacteria or stale urine).

Darcy is still afraid of electricity and still threatens to set sleeping people on fire who flirt with her (which explains why JJ sleeps with a fire extinguisher).

Joey is still our resident genius, except for the part of believing the world is flat.

Nelson is still our walking encyclopedia.

Chloe is still shy and super sweet. She still blurts out things that don't make sense (until later, when no one is paying attention). Well, no one but me. I pay attention to everything she does though, of course, I don't let on.

So, with all our unique personalities, you can see why it's hard to believe Max when he says were not nuts. But there is one thing we do believe. . . Each of us is God's favorite child. After all, that's what the fortune cookies told us, and why would fortune cookies lie?

Oh, and there are the dreams. I know they're weird and Dr. Aadil would probably say it's mass hysteria or something, but everyone of us has had some sort of dream where Trashman breathes on us, or kisses us, or gives us mouth to mouth resuscitation – just like he did with Max and Chloe.

"Hey, Dough Face!"

I turned to see Saffron rounding the cement wall

and stalking towards me. For the briefest second I caught a glimpse of her robe, the one covered in diamonds and emeralds that she doesn't like me to talk about since it's just my craziness.

"What the (*insert expletive here*) you doin', you stupid (*insert another expletive*)."

Saffron likes her expletives.

I scooted down the steep concrete bank until I could stand. "Good morning, your highness."

"Stop callin' me that! What you doin' here?"

I shrugged. "Freeway Scrabble."

She shouted something I couldn't quite make out over a belching truck.

I glanced down at the freeway and quickly pointed. "Look! See the middle lane? See the car being tailgated by the other two, and then the space, and then that little Volkswagen adding the dot? See how it makes the letter 'i'?"

She started to look then caught herself. "Get the (*expletive*) out of sight. If you see the (*expletive*) cars, they can see you!" She turned and without another word, or expletive, headed back toward camp.

I followed. "Sorry," I said."

"(*Expletive! Expletive!*)" she said.

Then, just before we rounded the wall, I glanced down at the freeway one last time. Sure enough, there it was again. A long eighteen wheeler in the left lane with two cars, side by side in the next two lanes at its back, two more cars, side by side, at its middle, and two more at its top. Together, just like they had so many times before, they made the final letter . . . a perfect, capital "**E**".

CHAPTER TWO

D
R

A
A
D
I
L

"I just hope somebody catches them before they burn down my house, or another hospital, or who knows what!"

I stared at the blue haired woman on the TV in my kitchen/living room/ bedroom/family room (I shared the bathroom with two other tenants down the hall). She was from the latest batch of street interviews the local stations were airing. Immediately following her was some balding, comb-over with too much cream filling around the edges:

"With that many religious crazies on the loose, who knows what they're capable of!"

I stared down at my hands holding a mug of tea. The liver spots formed a Rorschach pattern that seemed to grow daily.

"We're stalking up on pepper spray and we have a baseball bat under every bed."

Three days ago the fire at Sisco Heights Mental Health Facility had been the talk of the town. But that was old news. Now it was all about the eight patients who had escaped. Forget the loss of property or the loss of life (they had not yet found the janitor presumed to have died in the inferno). Now it was all about the, "crazed escapees and what they'd do next." The media had turned them into this week's main attraction, scaring the older citizens and creating outlaw heroes for the younger.

"I just want to know why they haven't been caught yet."

I glanced back at the screen to see a fashionably unshaven forty-something.

"It's been, what, three days now and nobody's seen them? Sounds pretty suspicious to me."

I swore under my breath and took a sip of the tasteless, green tea – another perk of old age and having the cholesterol level of a cheeseburger.

The off-screen reporter asked, *"Are you suggesting it's some sort of conspiracy or cover up?"*

"Wouldn't be the first," Forty-Something said.

Everything was a conspiracy these days. A remnant hangover of the Religious Wars and of Big Brother still stepping in from time to time to keep the peace.

"And if it's not a conspiracy?" the reporter asked.

"What then?"

"Then some heads better start rolling and they better start rolling fast."

I pushed the tea aside. What I wouldn't give for a cigarette. Of course the secondhand smoke laws had banned them years ago. And since I didn't like what medical marijuana did to my head, there was nothing I could legally light up.

My cell phone vibrated for the thousandth time, and for the thousandth time I ignored it. There was a chance it was my employer from Religious Affairs, but I had my doubts. He'd already decided how best to throw me under the bus.

I turned back to the TV, waiting in anticipation. The best was yet to come. And believe me, it would come. I'd seen it a dozen times, but couldn't wait for it again. It was like watching the reoccurring clip of a car wreck or some tornado destroying a building . . . over and over again.

Then, right on cue:

"Doctor! Doctor Aadil! Carrie Phillips, KBBS News!"

I stared at the screen and saw my own self exiting from the freight elevator of the Public Service Building. I'd been told there would be no press in this part of the garage. Apparently, the ambitious blonde reporter and her eager cameraman didn't get the memo.

"Doctor, is it true that they were ALL your patients?"

I'd served my country twenty years, been on two dozen covert operations, gone hand to hand with some of the baddest bad guys in the world, yet there I stood like a deer caught in headlights. When I finally found my voice, I managed to babble, *"What . . . who . . . I'm sorry?"*

"The Sisco Heights Eight."

"The . . . what did you call them?"

Like every other time I watched, I felt my stomach knotting up.

"Is it true you opposed transferring their ringleader, Maxwell Portenelli, to Sacramento where he could be watched more carefully?"

"I—"

"That you chose to keep him here, where security was more lax?"

Whoever had leaked the information made sure nothing was left out.

I watched myself lowering my head and muttering, *"Excuse me,"* as I quickly strode to my cramped little hybrid. It was only twenty feet away, but every step was hampered by the cameraman who kept blocking my path. *"Excuse me. Excuse me!"*

The kid didn't give an inch. For the record, I really didn't hit him. More like shoved, with some extra elbow action to the ribs just to make my point. Unfortunately, he made his own by stumbling backwards and falling hard to the garage floor. I couldn't tell if he was overacting for a lawsuit or if he was just that clumsy. Either way, the reporter screamed and ran to his side.

In the old days I might have gingerly planted a boot into his solar plexus to seal the deal before racing to my car. But with old age comes wisdom . . . and slower reflexes. I hobbled to the vehicle and counted myself lucky just to find the remote button on my keys. Once inside, I didn't bother to look over my shoulder. I started the car and took off, the wheels squealing on the smooth concrete. Had I bothered to look, I would have seen Blondie picking up the camera and videotaping my getaway. A getaway her TV station aired as often as possible, and that had already gone viral on the internet.

My cell phone vibrated again.

I may not be on the run like Maxwell Portenelli and friends, but I'd become equally as famous.

CHAPTER THREE

S
A
F
F
R
O
N

JJ, he figures the big landfill out here in the mud flats ain't a bad place to scavenge, 'specially with our new, celebrity, house guests. "Many hands make many bucks," he says, and he ain't wrong. 'Sides, no cop in their right mind would come lookin' for anybody out here with all the garbage, sewage and other surprises waitin' down in the muck and mire. Which probably 'splains why JJ says he got unfinished business to attend to in town. My man's pretty smart. Brandylin, my fourteen year old, says she's got to help him, so she's gone, too. Guess I'm surrounded by smart people.

'Cept for the crazies.

I ain't complainin'. They doin' pretty good diggin' through the garbage to find resalables and recyclables. Well 'cept Mariposa, our 6' 2" transvestite/nanny. She's terrified a germs (and breakin' a nail). Course, the crazies got their own germaphobe . . . some white haired nut job by the name a Winona who wears aluminum foil round her neck and says she's from another planet. This mornin' she's wearin' a hospital mask which cuts down the smells, 'cept for when she's got to remove it to hurl. Lucky we had slim pickins for breakfast so she's pretty much out of flying projectiles.

Then, a course, there's Dough Face who never stops talkin' and is definitely missin' a few candles on the cake. Serious, if he jabbered as much as he worked, we'd be millionaires:

"Hey fellas, check out this Happy Meal toy. Hey guys, check out this used toothbrush. Hey everyone, let's tell those knock-knock jokes again."

Forget candles, the dude's even missin' the cake.

Fortunately, no one pays him much mind, 'cept the shy, Asian chick and, a course, their leader, Mr. Kind Eyes. Seems he's got somethin' positive to say 'bout everyone. Even tried his juju on me by agreein' with Dough Face that I'm s'ppose to be some sorta queen or somethin'.

"City got enough queens," I say.

But he keeps goin' on 'bout how special I am, 'til I finally tell him to shut up, which he finally does. But you can't shut up that smile . . . or them eyes.

Other than that, they a pretty good crew. Still, I could do with a little less philosophizing and a little more work. Seems like they always discussin' somethin'.

Today was no different . . .

"Señor Max?" It was the crazy Hispanic with the bath towel, shower cap and goggles. Raphael something-something-something, the III. "I am afraid I still do not fully understand."

Kind Eyes looked up from the plastic bag he'd been diggin' in. "What's that, Ralphy?"

"If I truly am a superhero . . . why am I such a failure?"

"Who says you're a failure?"

Mariposa scoffs quietly and adjusts her tube top. "Look around you, honey. We're not exactly what you call cream of the crop."

"You are in God's eyes."

Mari snorts. "Then might I suggest this God of yours needs glasses because he is seriously blind."

Kind Eyes shook his head. "No. He just has better eyesight than you do."

"I am sorry, Señor Max, but I still do not understand."

Señor Max gave another smile. "God doesn't keep records of our wrongs, Ralphy. Remember? They were destroyed by Trashman. We're new people now, the old ones are gone."

Nelson, the kid with the photocopy brain, tilted his head and quoted, "Old things are passed away; behold, all things are become new."[1] Where he gets his stuff, who knows, but he's like their own, private Wikipedia.

"If I am so new," the caped crusader said, "why do I keep thinking and doing such bad things?"

Joey, a smart black kid who's pretty normal, 'cept for believin' the earth is flat, quipped, "Old habits die hard."

Senor Max nodded. "And that's all they are . . . habits. They're not you, Ralphy. They're just habits from the past."

"Muscle memory," Joey adds.

"But how do I stop them? These habits?"

"You can't. That's God's job."

Ralphy frowned and adjusted his goggles.

"Remember the diagram we drew back at the hospital?"

Dough Face chimed in. "The one with all the circles?"

Max nodded. "Remember the tiny seed in our center? How it stays dormant until God's Spirit enters it and gives us life?"

"That is the part I understand the least."

"Actually," Joey the brain said, "it's much like the fertilization process."

They all turned to him, waitin' for more.

"Like how the human egg has all that potential locked inside it, but nothing happens until it is fertilized."

"Ooo," Mariposa flipped back his hair. "A sex metaphor. I like that,"

Butch Babe, the one with all the tattoos, says, "Terrific. As if I don't got enough kids. Now I'm pregnant with God's?"

"They're coming!" the Asian chick shouts.

I spin round, but ain't nobody in sight. In fact, none of the others even seemed concerned.

Winona, the white-haired "extraterrestrial," says, "If we have become pregnant from God, how does this new life form improve one's behavior?"

"I'm guessing it's like any other newborn," Max

with the kind eyes says. "As long as we feed and care for it, it grows."

"But what do you feed an eternal God?" Ralphy asks.

Max shrugged. "Eternal food?" He paused, thinking. " . . .His eternal words, His eternal presence."

"So this baby, it's like a hybrid," Joey says.

"Hybrid?" Butch Babe asks.

"God's Spirit and ours, mixed together."

Max smiled. "I like that. And by feeding the new God/man hybrid with God food . . . we wind up being more like God."

Nelson tilted his head and quotes, ". . .that through these you may be partakers of the divine nature . . ."[2]

Everyone got real quiet. For a moment there's only the buzzin' flies which, believe me, is enough. Then I heard it, so faint it's probably just the breeze. But for a second it sounds like that flute music I heard the night of the hospital fire. It goes away as soon as it comes.

The caped crusader, clears his throat. "So . . . instead of looking back at the old me, I am to think on the new."

Max nodded. "That's right. There's no rehab program for corpses, Ralphy, so stop trying to change the dead one. Just focus on God and let Him do the heavy lifting."

You could see relief flood Ralphy's face. Max grinned right along with him. "He doesn't see what you were, only what He's making you. And Raphael Montoya Hernandez III?"

"Señor?"

"He's really, *really* impressed."

Ralphy can't help but giggle. Everyone else was smilin' pretty big, too, like they're all relieved.

'Bout then some lady's voice calls out, "That's quite a speech."

We spin 'round to see JJ and Brandylin comin'. They got some blonde bimbo reporter and cameraman with 'em.

Instantly, Ralphy leaps forward and shouts, "Stand back!" He lowers his goggles and yells to us, "Flee! I shall hold them at bay until you reach safety!"

"Relax," JJ says. "Ain't nobody here but us." He's slippin' and slidin' on the garbage, but for the most part manages to stay on top – a lot more than Bimbo and her friend can do.

"JJ!" I say. "We agreed, ain't nobody turnin' nobody in 'til–"

"Relax, babe. I ain't turnin' nobody in." He motions to Bimbo. "She don't know where our camp is. I'm jes lettin' her ask a few questions out here, that's all." He flashed a wad a bills from his pocket. "For a little spare change."

"Which is our little secret," the reporter says, pullin' her foot out of some ankle-deep muck.

The crazies were all pretty nervous, 'til they look over and see Max jes standin' there, doin' his smiling thing.

The reporter takes a couple wobbly steps closer. "Are you Maxwell Portenelli?"

He nods. "And you are . . ."

"Carrie Phillips." She waves away a swarm of flies. "From–"

"KBBS!" Dough Face shouts. I turn to see he's practically dancin' a jig. "I watch you all the time on

TV! Well, I mean when we had a TV. You're really pretty." (You can tell it ain't no come on, jes the way his mouth runs without botherin' to check with his brain).

She flashed her perfect tooth smile at his perfectly glazed eyes. Then she turned back to Max "So, tell me, Mr. Portenelli."

The cameraman stepped closer.

"Are you in any way affiliated with O.R.B.?"

"I'm sorry?" he says. "O.R.B.?"

"It's obvious you've cooked up quite the religion here. I'm just curious if—"

"Actually," he gives that smile of his, "it's not a religion."

"No?" She waved off the flies which seemed more attracted to her multiple coats of hair spray than the muck on her feet.

He shook his head. "Not even close."

"What would you call it then?"

He thought a moment, then answered. "A marriage."

"A marriage?"

He nods. "A supernatural union . . . between man and God."

"I see." 'Course she don't see, but it don't matter. "And why is that? What's the purpose of this . . . union?

"The purpose?"

"Yes"

"Why, to create new life."

"I'm sorry?"

"That's been His purpose all along." He turns from the girl to the cameraman. I gotta say, for a crazy, he sure believes his stuff. Then again, maybe that's what makes him crazy. He looks straight into the camera and without battin' an eye, says: "God wants to create a new life form. Within each of us. He wants to birth a brand new species never before witnessed in the history of the world."

CHAPTER FOUR

B
E
R
N
A
R
D

We're doing it again. Just like my other dream. Rolling down that big grassy hill. Me, Max and Trashman. I'm laughing so hard I'm crying. All I see is grass and sky, grass and sky, grass and sky. Max is in front of me, and Trashman is in front of him, hollering and whooping it up, having the time of his life – which I didn't have the heart to tell him had ended a few days earlier.

So there we were, rolling down the hill and running up to the top of it and rolling down again, and running up to the top of it – so dizzy we could barely stand, staggering around like we're drunk (which, honest, has never happened) or like someone had mistakenly given me the wrong meds (which *does* happen). On the third roll they came to a stop at the bottom, but for some reason I just kept on going.

"Atta boy, Bernie!" Max shouted as I rolled past them. "Go for it!"

Trashman clapped. "*Vaya! Vaya!*"

And *vaya* I did, until I suddenly ran out grass and sky . . . and everything else for that matter – well, except for water, which is just the sort of thing you'd find in a big river. I don't want to complain, because it's my own dream and I know I'm supposed to take responsibility, but I didn't remember any river being there before.

Still, it was pretty funny. As I splashed in and sank to the bottom like a stone I laughed all the harder, which is never a good idea when you're trying to breathe. The good news is I didn't drown. Somehow I managed to fight my way back to the surface. But once I got there, I did more than your minimum daily requirement of coughing, gagging and choking.

"Atta boy, Bernie!" Max shouted.

"*Bueno!*" Trashman laughed.

I tried to join in, but I was still a little concerned about the drowning part. The fact I didn't know how to swim didn't help. But, being a good sport, I happily waved while I desperately screamed, "HELP ME! HELP ME, HELP ME!"

Max didn't seem to understand. And Trashman just pulled out his flute thingie and began playing that airy little song of his.

"Guys! (*cough, cough*) I can't (*gag, gag*) swim (*choke, choke, choke*)!

"You're doing fine, Bernie. Just remember to–"

I slipped back under the water – kicking and waving my arms like a crazy man, which, as you know, I've had lots of experience at. When I accidentally bobbed back to the surface, I caught a glimpse of them strolling along the grassy bank.

"Max!" I shouted.

"Stop fighting."

"What?"

"Relax. Don't fight the water."

This, of course, made me fight all the harder, which made me sink all the faster. That's when I went from my regular panic mode to the *I'm-going-to-die-and-I-never-told-Chloe-that-I-loved-her* mode. My heart pounded in my ears. My lungs burned for air. I had to get back to the surface! But where did they put it? Everything was getting whiter and whiter. And then, just before I came down with a good case of unconsciousness, I popped back to the surface, doing my coughing and gagging thing.

"Max!"

Max and Trashman just stood on the bank, smiling away.

"Help me!"

"Stop fighting, Bernie. Let yourself go."

"What?!"

"Relax into it."

"That's crazy!" To prove my point, I slipped back under the water and tried drowning again. When I failed, I shot back up to the surface.

"You've got to become friends with it," he called.

"With the water?"

"That's right."

"It wants to kill me!"

"Because you're fighting it. Stop fighting."

Trashman nodded and continued to play his music.

"Relax, Bernie. Slow down and find the joy in it."

"In dying?"

"No, in the moment. Relax and take a deep breath."

Since my approach wasn't working as good as I hoped, I tried his. With nothing to lose but my life, I took a slow, deep breath–

"That's it," Max shouted. "That's–"

–and immediately sank, kicking and thrashing all the way, until I somehow clawed back to the surface. "I don't think (*cough, cough*) that's (*choke, choke*) helping."

"Try it again. Deep breath. Don't fight it. Be its friend."

I took another breath, even slower, and tried even harder. But the water didn't appreciate my efforts and kept trying to drag me under.

"No, don't fight. Don't fight it."

I took another breath, even deeper, and slowly stopped my arms from waving
in every direction.

"That's it. That's good, Bernie."

Ever so gradually, I quit thrashing.

"Great! Now take another breath. Slow and deep."

Things were getting a lot better without all that bothersome water rushing into my lungs. So I took another breath. And another. And before I knew it I was floating.

"Terrific! You're doing great!"

And he was right. For the first time in my life I was actually swimming . . . well, at least not drowning. And the deeper I breathed, the more I relaxed. And the more I relaxed, the more my panic disappeared. So did the pounding in my ears. Pretty soon, the only thing I heard was the roar which I hadn't noticed before.

"What's that sound?" I called.

"You're really going to have fun now," he shouted.

The roar grew louder.

"Fun?" I yelled. "Is that what this is?"

"And you thought rolling down that hill was exciting."

"I'm sorry," I shouted. "I can barely hear you."

"Just wait until you do this!"

"Do what?"

If he answered, I didn't hear because, suddenly, I was no longer floating in water. That's the good news. The bad news was I was floating in air, with the water a hundred feet below me! I'd just shot off a waterfall!

"Max!" I started to fall. "MAX!"

Suddenly, a pair of arms wrapped around me. "Right here," he said, "I'm right here."

"Where are–what's going–"

"Right here, Bernie. I'm right beside you."

I bolted up from my sleep, wide awake. The roar of the waterfall dissolved into the roar of the freeway. Everyone in camp was asleep, except for me and Max who was holding me.

"Are you okay?" he asked.

I nodded, still breathing hard.

"You sure?"

I nodded some more and he finally let me go. "Were you in the river?"

I turned to him in surprise.

"The waterfall?"

I nodded.

"Good." He smiled. "That's good."

I wanted to point out this was definitely a new definition of 'good,' but I only managed another nod.

He smiled and laid back down on his cardboard mat like he really expected to go back to sleep.

But sleep was the farthest thing from my mind. I just sat there amidst the roar of the early morning traffic. And, though I'm sure it was just a leftover from my dream, for the briefest moment I thought I heard Trashman's flute.

CHAPTER FIVE

A
L
E
X
I
S

"Alexis? Hey . . ." Someone was shaking me. "Lex, wake up."

I had no idea who, what or where I was. Proof of another great night of partying.

"Lex?" I felt a hand against my face, brushing aside my hair. Then a kiss on my cheek. "It's nine o'clock."

I tried answering but the piece of leather that had once been my tongue wasn't helpful. "AM . . . PM?"

Another kiss. I turned away so my breath wouldn't melt whosever face it was. The movement sent jackhammers exploding in my temples and pounding in my eye sockets.

25

The voice moved across the room. "My driver's waiting. I left a couple lines on the kitchen counter. Sprite's on the nightstand beside you with Tylenol." (For the uninitiated Sprite is great for hangovers though usually best to consume during binging, not after – while the blow, of course, is best for everything).

I heard the door open. "You were fantastic."

I tried raising a hand, settled for a thumbs up.

"See you soon." The door shut.

Eyes still closed, I patted the bedding until I realized with relief it was my quilt. I was in my apartment. As consciousness continued surfacing, so did my sense of accomplishment. The voice belonged to Troy Hudson. I had finally landed the god of physical perfection. I don't know where, I don't know how – but I had succeeded. Lying in bed, savoring the victory – just me and the marching band in my head – I heard the faint chatter of a TV set. I reached for the Sprite, but it was unopened and I didn't have the ambition to pursue. I was, however, able to unscrew the Tylenol bottle and pour them into my mouth like so many after dinner mints.

That's when I heard my name on the TV: *"Portenelli . . ."*

I pried open an eye, winced at the morning sun and found the TV. They were interviewing my father! I sat up, head exploding, stomach churning. I found the remote and turned it up. Some blonde reporter was talking:

"So you're telling everyone that not only is there a God, but that he's on their side?"

The camera cut back to Father. He stood in a giant field of mud. His fellow fugitives from the hospital were behind him. He was unshaven and his hair was disheveled from the wind. But even in my state, I could see how relaxed he was – hands in his pockets, smiling away. Nothing like the man I knew.

"Not only is He on our side," he said. "But He adores us. He yearns and longs for us."

"You mean sexually?" the reporter asked.

"Excuse me?" he said.

"Isn't that what you were just telling your disciples? That they need to have sex with their god?"

It was an obvious set up, but when they cut back to him, Father was still calm. In fact, his smile just grew bigger as he shook his head. "First of all, they are not my disciples. We're all learning as we go. And secondly–"

Darth Vader's Death March rang on my cell – Brother Robert's, ringtone. It was no doubt another emergency at the studio, which I'd normally ignore. But this was our father.

I found the phone near a pillow and answered. "Robert, channel 54."

"I'm watching it."

"They've found him?" I asked.

"No."

"But–"

"They won't reveal his location."

I stared at the TV, feeling a lump grow in my throat. "He looks . . . good."

"He looks atrocious. He'd never be caught wearing that ensemble. And the hair? Seriously?"

"I'll call later." I hung up without waiting for an answer.

The picture switched to some grubby handwriting on a piece of paper as the reporter's voice continued:

27

Anderson Public Library
114 N. Main
Lawrenceburg, KY 40342

"–believe that making a list of their failures and burning it will somehow bring absolution. Religious experts say such practices are a throwback to older beliefs and there is fear that the practice will spread among the more naive."

The picture cut back to Father speaking directly to the camera. "God wants to create a new life form. Within each of us. He wants to birth a brand new species never before witnessed in the history of the world."

Then back to the reporter. "This is Carrie Phillips reporting for KBBS."

And finally back to the newsroom where a couple constipated anchors sat.

He: "Very disturbing. Thank you, Carrie."

She: "Officials have asked for any viewer who may know the whereabouts of

Maxwell Portenelli and his group to contact the Department of Religious Affairs at area code 510-"

Darth Vader rang again and I picked up.

"Can you believe it?" Robert said.

"Yeah." I rubbed my head, calculating the odds of making it to the coke on the counter without puking. "Think they'll find him?"

"Let's hope."

I sighed. "Yeah."

"Listen, I have some news on Vittoria Haven."

That was it for Father. At least for now. It's not that we didn't love him, it was just– alright, maybe love is too strong of a word. But we respected him. How can you not respect a man who raised a fashion business from a garage boutique to one of the best known lines in the world? Of course the long hours and grueling pressures took its casualties in the parental department. It's not that he was mean or neglectful. He always performed his fatherly duties. Unfortunately, that's all they were. *Duties*. And, as dutiful children, Robert and I followed in his footsteps.

"So did we get her?" I asked. "Vittoria?"

"Remember that picture commitment she had in Germany?"

My stomach churned a little harder. "What about it?"

"They postponed the shoot until Spring."

"And?"

He didn't answer.

"Spill, Robert."

"She's agreed to be our lead model for the New York Show."

"Yes!"

"Oh, and one other minor point . . ." I could hear the tease in his voice.

"Robert . . ."

"I don't know if I should bother you with this now."

"Stop."

"Well, alright. She and Vogue have reached an agreement that she'll also be the model for our cover shoot."

"A two-for?" I leaped from bed. "The show *and* the cover!

I would have continued our conversation, but with the white, Berber carpet in my room, I felt it best to race to the loo to continue the festivities . . . driving the porcelain school bus between celebratory cries and gagging, gut-retching.

CHAPTER SIX

B
E
R
N
A
R
D

"Chloe, are you alright?"

Sweet, shy Chloe nodded her head yes, but her eyes were definitely saying no.

We'd been talking to one of our brand new street friends. We've been making lots of them lately. Friends, I mean. As soon as they see we're new to the streets and that we don't know what we're doing, everyone wants to help. It's great to have such thoughtful and friendly people. The guys are especially nice when Chloe is with me, which makes it a lot easier for us to share the neat thing that JJ thought up which I'll tell you about in a minute.

It's been almost a week since Max started showing up on the internet. We never plan it or anything. It just happens when someone on the street recognizes him and asks a question. And since he's way too nice to ignore them, he always tries to answer. Pretty soon others start gathering around and, before you know it, someone's recording him on their cell phone or texting their friends until a whole crowd begins showing up. Of course when that happens he can't stay too long because the police would find out and arrest him since he talks about God's love which, as you can imagine, is pretty controversial.

The other thing that's really been catching on is how folks are making out their lists and burning them just like we did with Trashman at the hospital. Thanks to JJ's neat plan, we go out onto the streets from morning to night and sell special paper that they can write their lists on. (For those who don't know how to write, we help out for a slight, additional charge). Then we bring the lists back to JJ where he burns them every night.

The first night we filled up a whole bucket and burned it right out on the street where lots of people could watch and video it. The next night, because of word of mouth and reoccurring clientele, we filled an entire shopping cart and burned it. A couple nights later we were up to two shopping carts. Then three. JJ says he wants to build a franchise to help everybody in the city. That's a lot of shopping carts, but by the happy look on everyone's faces, we're glad to help. And by the happy look on JJs face, he's really glad we're glad.

Oh, and there's one other thing. Some way, and don't ask me how, the shopping carts are starting to catch fire all by themselves. JJ doesn't even have to light them. He just collects the lists, fills up the carts and shoves them out onto the sidewalk. Pretty amazing, but sometime in the middle of the night, they just catch fire and burn up. Of course some one has to be doing it and there's lots of rumors that it's Trashman's ghost or something. Whoever it is, they're sure good at not getting caught.

But I digress . . . again.

So me and Chloe were talking to this new friend who, because of the cold drizzle, wore a plastic trash bag with holes cut out for his arms and head. He seemed nice enough, but I could tell Chloe thought there was something wrong.

"What is it?" I asked.

She shook her head.

Our friend could tell, too. "Come on, sweet cheeks," he said before breaking into a coughing fit. When he came up for air, he wheezed, "What's up?"

Chloe just looked away.

He gave her a grin which, considering his dental hygiene, may not have been his most attractive feature. But suddenly I understood. I'm not sure how, but someway the pattern of bare gums and blackened teeth told me a lot. It told me about his father doing unmentionable things to his sister and the way he tried to defend her which is how he lost the first tooth. But there were other things. Like the time he was in juvenile jail and some boys got him alone and, well, let's just say little sisters aren't the only ones unmentionable things are done to. Goodbye tooth number two, hello broken nose number one.

I don't want to make you nervous or anything, but my seeing things was happening more and more. Max keeps saying God's got a reason for making us the way we are. That our "uniqueness" may have gotten a little confused along the way, but deep inside, it's still from God . . . like Ralphy wanting to be a superhero, or Chloe seeing twenty seconds into the future, or Joey believing the earth is flat. Even Max's trips to Heaven. It's like each of these are gifts that God wants to fix up and grow in us.

But I'm digressing again.

So Chloe kept looking away until our friend finally said, "If you got somethin' to say, just say it."

She gave me a nervous look. I smiled and nodded for her to go ahead. She turned to face him though her eyes stayed somewhere on his chest. Her voice was small and soft. But not her words. "You are a very sick man."

"Chloe," I said.

He cocked his head, waiting for more.

She took a breath and continued. "She's twelve years old."

"Whoa, whoa, whoa." Our friend broke into another fit of coughing. "What you talkin' 'bout?"

I could see she'd started to tremble. But she took another breath and, still staring at his chest, answered, "The girl you are about to sleep with."

More coughing. "I ain't havin' no sex with no girl. 'Sides she's eighteen."

Chloe forced herself to look up until they were face to face. That's when I saw her tears.

But he just stared back, his own eyes cold, like some dead fish. "You crazy, girl." He laughed and shook his head

She blinked but didn't look away.

"Certifiable."

I saw his right cheek twitch so I stepped a little closer. Not to fight him. I don't know the first thing about fighting, but if I got between them maybe he'd wear himself out beating me up before he got to her.

He looked at me. Then back at her. Finally, muttering with a potty mouth as bad as Saffron's, he turned and limped down the alley. But not before leaving us with what I'm sure he thought was some helpful advice:

"If she know what's good for her, tell yer girlfriend to mind her own business."

It took a moment for me to come to (with Chloe being called my girlfriend and all), but when I did, I raised my pad and pencil and called after him, "Don't you want to make out that list?"

He just kept walking.

CHAPTER SEVEN

D
R

A
A
D
I
L

The view from the penthouse balcony was spectacular. Every light in the city was softened by the fog. The gauzy outline of the Bay Bridge grew more and more faint until it disappeared altogether into the gray blanket. Then, of course, there were the fires. Had I any doubt why I was really here, all I had to do was count the number of fires. There were nearly a dozen.

"That Maria, quite the cook, isn't she?"

I turned to see the honorable Rudolph Clark approaching. He was a handsome fifty-something, or an embarrassingly sixty-something, depending how the light reflected from his shiny, over-sculptured face.

"Yes she is," I agreed.

He arrived, breaking into a naughty-boy grin. "And believe me, that's not all she's good at."

I tried to smile. "And Mrs. Clark doesn't mind? The extracurricular activities?"

"Mind? She encourages it. Keeps me out of her hair . . . and drawers." He gave a throaty chuckle as he pulled a cigar from his jacket. I watched him clip off the end with a sterling silver cutter and hand it to me. "Cuban," was all he said. I took it and he prepared another. "I hear you're not a cannabis man."

"No sir."

"Me neither." He fired up a propane lighter and puffed on his cigar until it caught. Blowing the smoke over our heads he added, "Causes cancer."

He handed me the lighter and I followed suit. I closed my eyes and enjoyed the smell, the taste, even the feel as I rolled the contraband back and forth between my thumb and fingers. It had been a long time since I'd enjoyed this type of luxury – somewhere between my second and third wife.

We stood in silence, the faint sound of traffic drifting up from the street twenty stories below. I'd waited all night to officially hear why I, a lowly public servant, had been invited to this intimate dinner of half a dozen couples. I knew they needed a private pariah to keep their conversations going, but there was something else. After all, it was the Mayor. And, truth be told, I'd dropped out of the news cycle days ago. There was a new star on the horizon, Maxwell Portenelli. I'd only been his precursor, the voice of one crying in the wilderness.

"So how many do you count?"

"Sir?"

"Shopping carts?"

Here it came.

"Ten," I said. "Maybe twelve."

He nodded. "They say they're catching fire by themselves, now. Spontaneous combustion."

"Right," I pretended to chuckle.

"Folks pile the carts up with their lists, push them onto the street, and by morning there's nothing but ash." He took another puff and added, "Kind of like your hospital."

It was only the first salvo. I braced myself for more.

"So what are you doing about it?" he asked.

"The carts?"

"Your patients."

"Not much . . . unless you count searching the want ads for work." It didn't even raise a smile. I grew more serious. "There's nothing I can do. It's a police matter now."

"Unfortunately, the police are doing as good a job at finding them as you did in losing them . . . despite our Clean the Streets Campaign."

I turned to him in surprise. Clean the Streets was implemented just forty-eight hours earlier and its severity and racial profiling had already made headlines. The homeless were being arrested and fined for the smallest infractions – loitering, sleeping in public . . . as their camps were being systematically dismantled and destroyed. "That's all about him?" I asked. "Portenelli?"

"They're the ones hiding him and turning him

into this urban hero. The Campaign will put a stop to it soon enough. Crank up the heat 'til they cry uncle and hand him over."

"Sometimes persecution creates martyrs," I said. "Look what it's done for the Reverend and his organization."

The Mayor shook his head. "O.R.B. is small potatoes. This guy's a hundred times more popular . . . and dangerous."

I nodded. "Grass roots."

"Every time he opens his mouth he's on the internet. People are creating web sites for crying out loud. Thousands of hits a day."

I remained quiet as he took another puff and blew it into the air.

"You know him, Doctor. And his followers. Better than any of us, you know their strengths and weaknesses. You know what goes on in their unhealthy little brains. Surely, you can figure some way to bring them in."

"What about the State?" I asked. "With all the government surveillance can't they just—"

"This is a city matter. We don't need the State's help. We don't want the State's help."

"I'm sorry?"

"Politics is a delicate business, Doctor. Appearing weak empowers one's enemy."

I frowned. "This doesn't have anything to do with the upcoming gubernatorial race does it?"

"The one in which I'm a candidate? In which I've spent nearly four million dollars to reveal what an utter buffoon our current governor is? Why on earth would you suggest that?"

I closed my eyes and took a breath.

He looked back out over the city. "I know your record, Doctor. Your undying commitment during the Religious Wars."

"But—"

"The Department of Religious Affairs is run by children. Snotty-nosed youngsters that you, with all your wisdom and experience, have to answer to. Political appointees who've only read of the Wars, but have never lived them."

I waited for more.

"And, this November, should the state's power shift into more capable hands, well, I'm sure a man of your experience and dedication could be better recognized."

I looked at the lengthening ash of my cigar. "I appreciate that, but there's really nothing more I can do."

"I seriously doubt that."

"Sir?"

"With the Mayor's office behind you, you'll think of something. If you really put your mind to it."

I scowled. "I'm sorry. If the police can't do it, what you're asking of me is impossible."

"Impossible?"

"I think so."

"Well, keep thinking, Doctor. Think very hard."

His tone told me another shoe was about to drop. I wasn't wrong.

"Because there is another concern. Rumor has it, the district attorney is filing charges against you."

"Me?"

"Malpractice, reckless endangerment, and of course, accessory to murder."

"Murder?"

"The janitor, remember?"

"They've never found his body."

"Bodies are easy to come by."

I stared at him, absorbing the implications.

He took another puff. "When it comes to the carrot or the stick, I'm a big fan of the carrot, Doctor. But, as I've said, politics is a delicate business." He looked back out over the city. "One has to think long and hard before choosing one's friends . . . or enemies. And in using words like, 'impossible.'"

CHAPTER EIGHT

S
A
F
F
R
O
N

"I write that list. I give it to JJ. It magically burns up with the others . . ."

"And?"

"And nothin'. I tell God, 'Give me the goodies, do your God thing,' and still nothin'. I'm the same ol' me. 'Cept now, me and the old lady get our camp torn down. Cops come in and take everythin' and we got nothin!"

Max looked at the skinny dope fiend all lovin' like he really cares, which by now I know he does. Then he answers, "Real growth takes time."

"Growth?" The fiend starts coughin' 'til he hacks

41

up a big wad of phlegm. "We worse now than when we started!"

I looked over the crowd. We was already up to ten, maybe fifteen. I don't like it and know I gotta get us out a there.

Real gentle Max asks, "Are you feeding your spirit? Are you spending time thanking God?"

"Thankin' Him? For takin' my camp?" The fiend waved his boney arm at the alley which looked and smelled as bad as him. "For livin' like this?"

The place is a favorite hangout since there's plenty of restaurants in front which means prime dumpster divin' in back. 'Course I tried steerin' Max and two of his wannabes away from it since it's just off Mission Street and way too public. But one thing you can say 'bout him, he's as stubborn as he is naïve.

JJ says it's my job now, to protect the golden goose. Not that I mind. 'Specially since he ain't bringin' up the royalty thing no more. Least with his mouth. But there's still them eyes. I seen lots a men lookin' at me lots a ways. But never like that.

Now he's got them same eyes fixed on the dope fiend. "I don't think God expects you to thank Him for any of this."

The fiend snorts. "Good, cause there ain't no way in—"

"But . . . I think He wants you to adore Him in spite of it. He wants you to trust Him that He'll use it."

"Use *this*?" The doper motions down the alley and starts hackin' again. When he's through he says, "For what?"

"To continue the work He's started."

"Work? Where?"

"In you."

"Me?"

"He wants to make you bigger . . . greater. He wants to make you like Him."

I can see the veins in the fiend's temples bulge. He steps in closer. I step in too, jus' to let him know I'm there. "You tellin' me it's God's will I suffer like this?"

Max shakes his head. "No. What you see here is man's will, not God's."

"And your God, He ain't big enough to fix it?"

"Actually, He's bigger. He's so big that if you let Him, He'll turn all of this around and use it for your good."

"That's crazy talk."

"Yes it is."

Jimmy, the genius kid, weighs in, "Unless, of course, you're speaking of an infinite God of multiple-dimensions."

The fiend frowns. "You as nuts as him."

Jimmy sighs. "If only."

"Norm, look!"

We spin 'round to see some cracker tourist comin' at us from the street. There must be twenty of us standin' but she only sees Max. "It's you, right?" she says. "The prophet man?"

He jus' smiles at her.

"I knew it." She suddenly sees the rest of us and stops. "Is it safe?"

He keeps smilin' and gives her a nod.

She smiles back and shouts over her shoulder. "Norm, you won't believe this. Norman! Kids! Come here! Get out your phones."

Norman, a walkin' vat-a-fat, and his two mini-vats,

come round the corner. 'Fore I know it, they got their phones up and are gettin' way too close.

"Whoa." I raise my hands. "Back off. No pictures. It ain't him."

But Max just keeps smilin' and says, "It's alright."

I shoot him a look, but it's too late, they already crowdin' around, snappin' their pics.

"Oh, a group shot!" Mom cries, "Shannon, you stand there to his right. Jason, here, next to me." She moves 'em 'round like chess pieces, all the time chatterin'. "We're such fans. Norm, a little closer. We watch you all the time – Jason, a little cooperation wouldn't hurt – whenever there's a new post."

When everyone's set, she looks to me, hesitates, then hands over her phone. "Do you mind?"

I ain't happy, but I take it.

"Make sure you get us all in. And count."

"What?"

She talks loud and clear like I'm a idiot. "Count. You know, one, two, three."

"I know what count means you fat piece of–" I catch Max eyes and stop myself.

I raise the phone and take the pic.

"How was that?" she asks.

"Perfect," I say, tryin' not to snarl.

She takes the camera, obviously grateful I ain't pawned it yet, and starts

gushin'. "We just love your city. So diverse, so colorful. Especially you people." I give her a look and she quickly 'splains, "You know, living in these awful conditions like this. I think you're all so brave and so very courageous."

'Fore I get the chance to tell her what I think of *her* people, she presses a bill into my palm and smiles.

'Fore I decide whether to throw it in her face, or ask for more, she turns to her brood and motions for them to go. As they head off, she looks over her shoulder, thankin' us one last time, then waddles away, chattering to 'em 'bout what a privilege they just had, and how everyone should be more grateful.

When she's finally gone, the dope fiend picks up right where he left off. "You expect me to thank God for people like that?" He motions back to the alley, "For places like this?"

Max holds his gaze then quietly answers, "God never plays defense."

"What you talkin' 'bout now?"

"He only plays offense. He's so big that if you let Him, He'll use every bit of this ugliness for your good."

Nelson, who'd been quiet as a tomb, tilts back his head and quotes, "all things God works for the good of those who love him, who have been called according to his purpose."[3]

The fiend just glares at him.

That's when Franny, part time hustler and full time crack whore, steps in. Me and Fran, we been on the streets since childhood. This is the first she's heard Max and apparently she got some opinions of her own. "So why don't He do somethin'," she says. "Why don't God come down here and straighten things out?"

Max nods like she's got a point, then he answers. "I wonder . . . instead of asking God to come down into our lives . . . maybe we should ask Him to take us up into His."

The fiend swears. "More double talk."

Max shakes his head. "Not really."

45

"So what you sayin'?" Fran asks.

"I'm saying the key is to see things from His perspective . . . not ours."

Nelson rattles off somethin' else. "Be not conformed to this world but be transformed by the renewing of your mind."[4]

Max keeps goin'. "God loves you. More than you love yourself. And He desperately wants to free you."

"From what?" Fran says.

"From yourself. He wants to make you as free as He is."

"You're crazy."

"I believe we've already established that fact," Jimmy says.

Max pauses. He looks at the growin' crowd, then the alley. Finally, he turns back to Fran and the dope fiend. "All of this you see here, all of these trials, these hardships . . . they're simply a chisel. God didn't invent them, and He certainly doesn't approve of them. But He'll use them. He'll use them to chisel you and me out of our prisons. To unlock the glory trapped inside."

"Glory? What glory?"

"His."

The dope fiend sneers. "Glory . . . in me?"

Max nods. "He longs for us to be free, to be all He dreamed of when He thought of us. It's true, we all want to change our situations, but . . ."

"But what?"

"What if He wants to change us?"

A voice speaks up from the crowd, low and commanding. "Consider it pure joy, my brothers, whenever you face trials of many kinds—"

I turn to see a tall, mysterious fellow in a long coat.

As he approaches, I see he's good lookin' with good clothes. Definitely not one of us. I step a little closer, case he tries somethin'.

"–because you know that the testing of your faith develops perseverance. Perseverance must finish its work so that you may be mature and complete, not lacking anything." [5]

Nelson tops it off by sayin', "James 1:2-4."

We turn to Max who's been carefully listenin.'

But Mystery Man ain't done. He nods to Nelson. "As my young friend here previously quoted, the Ancient Text does not say, 'Consider it *some* joy.' Nor does it say, 'Consider it *mostly* joy.' Instead it clearly states that we are to consider our trials '*PURE* joy'."

Fran squints at him. "I seen you before."

He nods. "I get around."

"Who are you?"

"A friend."

We all stare a moment, 'til the dope fiend turns back to Max. "I'm okay payin' JJ to put my list in his shoppin' cart. I'm even good at believin' it somehow burns up. But thanking God for this?" He motions to the alley. "No way."

Max holds his gaze. You can see the compassion in his eyes. But the fiend don't back down.

"So God gonna stop lovin' me now? If I don't play by His rules and grovel and thank Him? You're gonna tell me He hates me now?"

Max slowly shakes his head. "God won't hate you. But you will."

The fiend don't like this much, but Max continues.

"You'll always hate yourself. And Him. You'll always play the victim. You'll never become 'mature.'" Max hesitates, then looks down. There ain't no missin' the sadness in his voice. "You'll never become the God-man He longs for you to be."

I see the vein in the fiend's head swell bigger. He breaks into more coughing and hacking. When he's done, he spits the wad on Max's shoe.

Max stands there, all quiet.

The fiend turns to the group. "He's a liar! A lunatic and a liar. And you're as nuts as him if you believe—"

Suddenly two squad cars appear, screechin' to a stop in front of the alley's entrance.

I grab Max's arm. "Let's go!"

"But—"

"Now!

He fights me jus' long enough for Mystery Man to slip a piece a paper in his hand 'fore I get him pulled away. And off we go down the alley, past the dumpsters and towards the other end. I hear shoutin' but we got a good start and I know my people will do their best to slow the cops.

We come out and veer 'cross Mission Street, then hook a right and disappear down another alley. Up ahead, a truck is at a loadin' dock. We duck round it outta site – me and Max wheezin' our lungs out, Jimmy and Nelson barely breakin' a sweat. I hate youth.

Jimmy motioned to the paper in Max's hand. "What's that?"

Max unfolds it and tries readin' without his glasses. "Looks like an address."

"To what?"

He squints at the paper makin' sure he got it right. "O.R.B." he says. "It's the address to something called, O.R.B."

CHAPTER NINE

B
E
R
N
A
R
D

Everyone was pretty excited about the group field trip to O.R.B. We hadn't been on one since we burned down the hospital. I really miss those days. At the hospital, I mean. Well, except for the surveillance cameras (which were okay if you didn't know where you were, but not so good if you wanted to be there by yourself), or the boiled food (which was okay for potatoes, but not so good for pies and cupcakes). Then, of course, there were our meds . . .

Jimmy and Nelson had been spending a lot of time researching our meds down at the library – Jimmy to look stuff up, Nelson to hold him in his chair in case he slid onto the wall or, worst yet, the ceiling. (Living on a flat earth has its disadvantages). They discovered our medication was good for your average, run-of-the-mill crazies, but not so good for us super-deluxe ones. Because of our religious issues, (Max called them gifts) we were given specific drugs to help suppress our episodes.

Sometimes they worked, sometimes they didn't.

For me, I still can't get a single inanimate object to talk to me. No stop signs, no parking meters, not even Darcy's tattoos. But patterns? My oh my, they're showing me stuff all the time. Sometimes I hear them in sounds, like a barking dog or the clatter of leaves. Other times I see them in clouds, used cigarette butts, even flea bites which, I don't want to complain, but in Saffron's camp, they could cut down a little bit on all their chatter.

Anyways, because the city officials were still cranky about us being criminals at large, and because JJ wanted us to keep selling those lists, he tried to discourage us from going. To the O.R.B., I mean. It was kind of heart-warming to hear all his rantings and ravings. Dr. Aadil says different people have different love languages and by JJ's vocabulary you could tell he loved us a lot.

But Saffron said it was okay and, in case you didn't notice, what Saffron says, usually goes. She'd never been to an O.R.B. meeting but if Max was invited she figured we all were. Well, except for Jimmy and Nelson who wanted to go back to the library. And JJ, who was visiting a local appliance shop that had just burned down. Even though he didn't know the owner, he was willing to step in and help clean up. Like I said, JJ's got a big heart.

Of all of us, Mariposa was the most excited. "The Reverend, he is such a huge celebrity," he said. "I can hardly wait to meet him." He turned to Saffron. "I'm surprised you didn't immediately recognize the man."

Brandylin, Saffron's fourteen year old daughter, nodded. "His picture is on all those flyers and tracts. A real hottie."

"You got that right, girlfriend." Mariposa fanned himself. "He could heat up my life anytime."

"Me, too."

"Brandylin!" Saffron scolded.

"What?"

"He's old enough to be your father. Your *grand*father."

"I like a man with experience."

Saffron cut her a look which wasn't all that friendly which was okay because Brandylin pretended to ignore it anyway.

We were about one block from the meeting place, which was in some back alley, when Ralphy spotted Winona's signal and raised his hand for us to stop. She was up ahead, using her intergalactic communicator lipstick case to determine if there was any hostile life forms or police officers in the area.

As we stood waiting, Ralphy turned to Mariposa, "The initials, O.R.B? What exactly do they stand for?"

Mariposa sighed dramatically. Everything he did was dramatic. Seriously, he could be a Broadway actor . . . or actress, he was that good. And he sure had the wardrobe to prove it. "As I have stated at least a dozen times, it is called the Order of Religious Believers. They are an uber-secret organization, *very* anti-government and a *very* big deal." Unable to restrain himself, he reached out to straighten Darcy's black, leather vest. "So, please, all of you, do your best to at least *pretend* to be normal."

Darcy glared at him and he stopped. The fact that she didn't hit him or break any body parts was a sure sign she was also getting better.

"So do you think there's a chance I could get his autograph?" I asked.

"Who?"

"The Reverend?"

Mariposa turned to me and blinked. "Honestly," he checked his hair in a passing store window, "did your parents conceive any children with brain activity?"

Before I could choose an answer, Chloe blurted, "He may be slow but you're the one who's. . ." She caught herself and stopped. We all looked at her. She pulled into her sweater like she always does when she's trying to disappear.

"What's that, child?" Mariposa asked.

She looked down and shook her head.

"Talk to me. What were you saying?"

I spoke up to defend her. "Sometimes Chloe, she says things that—"

"I'm not talking to you, butterball. I'm talking to her."

We all kind of waited, not sure what to say.

"Well?"

When it was clear Mariposa wouldn't let her off the hook, Chloe finally raised her head and said, "You're the one who's going to die of some STD."

If it was kind of quiet before, it was dead quiet now.

"Excuse me?" Mariposa said.

Chloe swallowed, then continued. "But you don't

have to. You can stop all your pretend silliness and get help."

I just stared. So did everybody else. But she wasn't done.

"No one here respects you. They act like it, but not really. Everyone thinks you're a joke. They won't say it to your face, but they do. We all do." She took a deep breath and glanced to me. Before I could recover, she looked back to the ground and gave her hair a shake to cover her face.

I glanced to Mariposa. He was turning fifty shades of red. Finally he said, "Well, do we feel better? Now that we've gotten all that off our tiny, little breasts?"

Chloe kept staring at the ground.

Mariposa turned to Maxwell. "Are you going to allow your little protégé, here, to talk to me in that manner?"

Max frowned, "I'm sorry. I don't know what to say."

"Really?"

He shook his head.

"Well, I do. The first word starts with 'good' and the second ends with 'bye.'" She turned back to Chloe. "I will not stand here and be spoken to like that. Especially by some crazy Asian with such a total lack of fashion sense. So, if you will excuse me." He turned around, adjusted the strap on his dress and started up the alley.

Saffron called after him. "Mariposa! Mari!"

But he just kept on walking, heels clicking on the concrete.

Slowly, one by one, we turned to Chloe. She shifted under our gaze then muttered, "Well, it's true."

I glanced to Max who was studying her thoughtfully. Finally he said, "Yes, Chloe, it is true. But it's not the truth."

"Let's go, people." Winona called and waved for us to join her on the other side of the street.

Ralphy nodded and motioned us forward.

"What's that s'pose to mean," Saffron said. "'It's true but not the truth?'"

Max paused to find the right words. "It's true, Mariposa has his problems. But it's not the truth. It's not how God sees him."

"How does God see him?" I asked.

"If Mariposa made out his list of failures, if he's burned them, then they no longer exist."

Ralphy nodded. "He is as you say, 'a new man.'" Then, a little softer, he added, "or whatever."

"So if his failures don't exist, what does?" I asked.

"The truth," Max said. "What God sees as His completed work in him."

"In Mariposa?" Brandylin said.

"If he's asked God's Spirit to come in and co-mingle with his, then God's truth is what God is focused on."

"But his clothes?" Ralphy said. "His makeup, his heels?"

"All areas of crippledness, the missing pieces God will heal and replace . . . if he lets Him."

"That's how God sees him?" I asked. "All healed and fixed up?"

Max nodded. "And that's the difference." He turned to Chloe. "When you see things, try to see them through God's eyes. That's the real truth. Instead of telling someone what's wrong with them—"

"As if Mari don't already know," Brandylin said.

Max nodded, "Instead of telling someone what they already know and hate about themselves – their shortcomings, their failures – a true prophet should tell them what they don't know."

Darcy asked, "Which is?"

"How deeply God loves them. The greatness He has planned for them."

"If they let Him," I repeated.

Max nodded. "After Trashman destroyed our records back in the hospital, what's true no longer matters. Now all that counts is the truth."

Ralphy added, "And truth is how God sees us."

"Exactly."

We finally arrived and joined Winona who stood at a closed, metal door. "Everyone ready?" she asked.

We all nodded.

"All right then." She pulled open the door. "Let's check this thing out."

CHAPTER TEN

A
L
E
X
I
S

"I don't understand."

"There is nothing to understand. If the clothes do not fit, they do not fit."

"Right," I said. "But maybe your people made an error in the measurements?"

"My people have been employed longer than your youngsters have been alive."

It was mid-morning and we'd already begun the pissing contest. Don't get me wrong, there's always friction in a cover shoot between the fashion designer and the fashion editor. But we're talking Natalie Falibrez. Natalie Falibrez who has more testosterone than the entire offensive line of the San Francisco

49er's. Some say she goes in for weekly treatments, which may be a little unfair. I'm sure all that body hair is naturally genetic.

I lowered my voice so not to be overheard by the fourteen-person crew who glanced away, suddenly busying themselves with work while, of course, straining to hear every syllable. "We used the measurements you sent. I think she's put on weight."

"Then find another outfit that is not so revealing. Really, Alexis, it is not that difficult."

"Our entire line is . . . form fitting."

Vittoria Haven, our movie star, model, and current migraine maker, called from the giant birdcage she'd been posing in, "Excuse me? Is there a problem?"

Natalie turned to her, all smiles and grace. "No dear, no problem at all. Listen, why don't you go back into the dressing room for a little while and take a breather."

"But, we've just begun."

"I know. But I see no need to concern you with the incompetency of others. In fact," she turned to the group and clapped her hands, "everyone, may I have your attention please? We shall be breaking for an early lunch. Julian? Where's Julian?"

An emaciated minion in spray-on jeans stepped forward. "It's Jonathan."

"Of course it is. Please, begin taking lunch orders. And Alexis?" She turned back to me. "You have exactly seventy-five minutes to solve this problem."

"Natalie, what am I–"

"I do not care how you do it. Ease them out. Find something that fits. Go back to fashion school." She glanced at her 18-Karot Imperiale. "If we have no solution by 12:10, I shall cancel the shoot and send everyone home . . . with your company footing the entire bill."

"Natalie—"

She turned and walked toward the door. "Seventy-five minutes, Alexis. Not a minute more."

The crew traded looks then busied themselves with their faux work.

Robert immediately joined me. "What's going on?"

"I don't know." I shouted, "Tommy! Sky!"

My assistants materialized on either side, quick with excuses to continue their employment:

"They're the same measurements they sent us . . ."

"Here's the FAX . . ."

"We've double-checked . . ."

"Well, check again." I pushed past them and headed down the hall for the dressing room Vittoria had practically raced to.

"Ms. Portenelli? Alexis?"

I turned to see Father's doctor standing beside the craft service table of juices, croissants, baguettes, and of course an abundance of coffee and sugar free Red Bull. Other stimulants were also available, though hidden from Natalie's less-tolerant eyes.

"What are you doing here?" I said. "How'd you get in?"

He washed down the last of his Danish with a gulp of coffee and approached, brushing crumbs from a cardigan that should have been in the Smithsonian. "I wonder if I might have a minute of your time."

I continued toward the dressing room. "Not now, Doctor."

"But, your father—"

"Not now."

Robert and I arrived at Vittoria's door. We exchanged looks, took a breath and opened it.

She sat with her back to us, facing the brightly lit mirrors. Already swollen-eyed, she did her best to hide her own Danish by sneaking it to the makeup artist beside her. Robert and I approached on either side.

"Sweetheart," I asked, "are you alright? Is everything okay?"

The makeup artist and her assistant took their cue and pulled away, melting into the back of the room.

"I'm so sorry," Vittoria said, clutching a tissue in her hand.

"No, that's okay," I said as I reached out and adjusted her collar. "What's going on?"

"They don't fit, do they? Nothing fits." She reached up to wipe her eyes. Robert and I both resisted the urge to stop her. Every wipe meant another twenty minutes in makeup.

"You've been under a lot of pressure," I said. "I know, because I eat tons when I'm nervous."

"And tons when she's not," Robert said.

Ignoring him, I asked, "What's happening?"

She looked at us in the mirror a moment then burst into tears.

"Vittoria? Sweetie." I knelt down and took her hand, making sure it was the one holding the tissue.

"I'm pregnant," she blurted.

I felt a wave of relief. "Oh, is that all. Don't worry, it happens to the best of us."

She nodded, trying unsuccessfully to raise the tissue to her face.

"Here, let me." I took it from her and carefully

BILL MYERS

dabbed the edge of her eyes with its corner. "We can easily postpone the shoot, right Robert?"

She sniffed. "You can?"

"Absolutely." Robert rose and reached for his phone. "We'll schedule you into a clinic this afternoon. You'll be good in no time."

"You don't understand."

"What's that, darling?"

"I'm . . . keeping the baby."

"You're what?" I looked to Robert who was equally confused.

"Winston and I have discussed it and we're keeping the baby."

"But . . . we've . . . I . . ."

Robert stepped in to translate. "Vittoria," he knelt back down to her, "we agreed."

"I know and I feel awful."

"Right, but . . . we've signed contracts."

She looked up, giving him her best doe-eyes.

The muscles in Robert's jaw tighten. My mind raced. This was not going well. Then I said, "Hold it, wait a minute, we'll be okay."

They looked to me.

"Sure. I can adjust the clothes. Ease them out a bit. We'll make it work."

"Alex . . ." Robert warned.

"I'm serious. We'll reschedule tomorrow before any more damage is done. We'll be fine."

"You'd do that?" Vittoria's voice squeaked with smallness.

I dabbed the rim of her eyes again, "For you, sweetheart, anything."

"Alexis."

I looked over to Robert.

60

"What about the New York show?"

The bottom dropped out of my stomach.

He turned to her. "The New York Fashion show is coming up in six weeks."

"I know," she said, "and I feel just terrible. I'm so very, very sorry."

"Sorry?" Robert said.

"Yes." She looked down, choking out a pathetic, little sob. I did mention she was a professional actress, right?

"You're under contract," he said.

"I know and I feel so bad. Just . . ." she took a quivering breath, "awful."

He continued, "Our entire line this season is based upon your appearance."

She nodded, tears filling those eyes.

But Robert was a pro, too. "This cover, the advertising, the New York show. Everything is about you, Vittoria. And . . . we have a contract."

Her voice trembled. "We'll return your money."

"It's not just the money," I softly said, "which by the way would cost millions. It's about our company. You'd be jeopardizing our entire company."

Robert continued, equally as kind. "That's why we have contracts."

She turned to him, tears spilling down that $110,000 a day face. "You would force me to have an abortion?"

He gently answered, "I didn't force you to get pregnant."

She turned to me. I nodded, trying my best to show solidarity. She turned back to Robert, her perfect mouth opening, then closing again. Her delicate lips pursing. And then, hissing more than speaking, she said, "How dare you."

We remained silent.

"We're talking about a life here. A human life."

Somehow, she found the strength to rise to her feet. And, unassisted by any scriptwriter, she tried to improvise. "We're talking about a living human life that's living. A sacred, little, baby . . . thing." (Improvisation wasn't her strong suit).

Suddenly the tears vanished. The muscles in her neck tightened. Then, with the greatest regal sovereignty, she said, "My lawyers shall be contacting you."

"Good," Robert said. "Terrific. We can all get together and discuss the court injunction we'll slap on you before the day ends."

"Get out!" She'd begun to tremble again. This time it looked real.

Robert motioned me toward the door. It seemed a good idea and I obeyed. He followed.

"Get out!"

We stepped into the hall and shut the door.

"Well?" I said.

Robert started down the hall. "We have contracts."

I joined him. "And lawyers."

"The best."

"Ms. Portenelli . . ."

I looked up to see Father's doctor standing at the end of the hall, coffee and another pastry in hand.

"Yes? What is it?" I said. "Have you heard anything?"

"No." He joined us as we continued through the studio.

"Then, what—"

"I have an idea. I've been talking with the Mayor and we think there's a way to draw your father out of hiding."

I scanned the room, grateful most of the crew had gone on break.

"We think there's a way to pull him off the streets and return him to hospital care."

"And how do you do that, Doctor? How are you going to succeed in something the police have completely failed at?"

"We'll succeed with you."

I slowed to a stop. "What?"

"I saw the way you connected with him back at the hospital. That's what will bring him out of hiding."

"What will?"

"You, Ms. Portenelli. You'll be the one to draw him out."

CHAPTER ELEVEN

S
A
F
F
R
O
N

"'The people of the land have used oppression, and exercised robbery, and have vexed the poor and needy: yea, they have oppressed the stranger wrongfully.'"[6]

With eyes shut, and quotin' from memory, The Reverend stood at front, his trimmed beard and good-lookin' features flickerin' in the candle light. There's no 'lectrical power down here. Plenty a cold and damp though. It's some big, forgotten cellar. Almost a cavern. And it's packed. Most every chair filled. Nearly all street people.

Earlier, we got to meet the Reverend, all six foot,

two of him. He remembered Max. Fact, towards the beginning of his speech, he pointed Max out to the crowd which got everyone to clap. Though he's educated, the man ain't stuffy like you'd expect. Just solid and sincere. The type you'd want in your corner. 'Course, Dough Face, who's an open book, (with mostly blank pages) did his usual fallin' all over himself when he got introduced. But the others weren't too bad – 'cept maybe Ralphy who stood guard at the bottom of the stairs, goggles in place, ready to defend against intruders. And Winona, who kept checkin' her tampon dispenser, 'fraid we was too far underground to get signals from the mother ship.

Other than that, we was fine.

And the speech he was given' was fine, too. Fact, the more he talked, the more it got me to thinkin' on what Max had been sayin' 'bout God and stuff.

"'Ye adulterers and adulteresses, know ye not that the friendship of the world is enmity with God? Whosoever therefore will be a friend of the world is the enemy of God.'"[7]

He paused and looked over the crowd. "And who is the enemy of God?" he said. "Friendship of the what?"

"The world," they shout back.

"That's right. It's any one who puts the world before God and this Ancient Text." He reached down and pats a waist-high safe beside him – one of them old-fashioned kind they used to drop on Wiley Coyote in the cartoons. It's closed and locked up tight. Then he quotes again, "'Draw nigh to God and he will draw nigh to you. Cleanse your hands, ye sinners; and purify your hearts, ye double minded.'[8] That's what it says."

The man's tough, but you can tell he's honest. Like he's tellin' the truth straight up – no sugar coatin' or butt kissin'.

"And here's another. He pats the safe again. 'God judgeth the righteous, and is angry with the wicked every day.'[9] "Every day, my friends. Not some days, not most days, but how many days?"

"Every day!" the crowd calls back.

"That's right. He is angry at them *every* day."

A few shout, "Amen." Others are noddin' like they're really gettin' it.

I glance to Max. He's listenin' real hard.

"'Be ye therefore perfect, even as your Father which is in heaven is perfect.'[10] That's what it says. Now, some are going to whine and complain, insisting that this is just too tall of an order to obey. But I tell you my friends, they are wrong. If it was too hard, God would never have commanded it."

He begins pacing back and forth. "Granted, it is not easy . . . but it is not impossible. Not for the dedicated. Not for those who are truly committed."

"Amen!" some more shout.

"But there is a secret. There is a clear and foolproof way of being holy. And it works every time without fail." He pauses, makin' sure he's got everyone's attention. I even catch myself leanin' forward.

"You do it by . . . doing it."

Chuckles ripple through the room, but he ain't kiddin'.

"You don't talk about it. You don't dream about it. You do it." He motions back to the safe. "Saying you're a follower of the Ancient Texts doesn't mean a thing. I can stand in a garage all day long and say I am a Mercedes Benz. But does that make me a Mercedes Benz?"

"No," the crowd calls back.

"That's right. The proof is in what I do. If I fire up my engine, if I pull out of the garage and roll down the highway, if I stop to get my oil changed, well then we got some proof."

More chuckles.

"The world is full of words without action. And they mean nothing. But words *with* action . . . well now, they mean everything. Saying I believe in God without proof means nothing. Just words – as dead and useless as that crate over there." He motions to a broken down crate near the front wall. "You want to be like that crate?"

"No," they shout back.

"Of course not. Because you're smarter than that crate." He shrugs. "Well most of you."

More laughter, includin' me.

"You're smarter than that crate because you are human beings. You are masters of your own destiny. Each and every one of you has free will. That's how God made you. You can choose to do right or you can choose to do wrong. You can choose success or you can choose failure. Riches or poverty. The decision is yours. Nobody else's. Yours and yours alone!"

He begins pacin' again. "Is it hard? Yes, it is. Harder than nails. But *you* have the choice. And *you* have the power!"

"That's right!" some shout.

I see his point. We all got a will. And we all can change, if we really want. It's just like Max says, we can be new people. It's just a matter of doin' it.

The Reverend keeps pacin back and forth, his voice gettin' louder. "And if all you find in those dumpsters out there is lemons, then what do you make?"

"Lemonade," they shout.

"That's right. Life can knock you down, but staying there or getting back up, that's *your* choice. *You* are the one with free will. *You* are the master of your destiny."

More shouts and amens.

"And don't expect hand outs. There are no free meals in God's soup kitchen."

More agreement, some clap.

"You can cry and moan all you want, but the truth of the matter is, God helps those who help themselves."

More applause. I ain't no pushover, but I'm definitely gettin' his point.

"So come. Join me. Fix yourselves. And with the help of God, let us fix this great nation. Together, let us throw off our oppressors, those who hold us down, those who say we cannot change. Because we can change! Together let us rise up with God and become a new people with a new life in a new country!"

The room begins to cheer.

"You can do it. You can change yourself. We can change this great nation. Yes you can. Repeat after me: I can do it!"

"I can do it," everyone shouts.

He cups his ears. "What?"

We shout louder, "I can do it!"

"I can't hear you."

The room yells, "I CAN DO IT!" and everyone

breaks into applause.

"This is not child's play. This is your life. Do you want to keep living a broken life serving a broken government in a broken world . . . or do you want to rise up and become a new man and new woman?"

The crowd cheers and continues clappin'.

"Alright then. Get to your feet. Choose this day who you will serve. Get to your feet and take a stand. Take a stand for God. Take a stand for your country. Take a stand for yourself!"

More clappin' and cheerin' as everyone gets up. Some, like Winona and Dough Face, practically leap from their chairs. Others, like me and Max, rise a little slower. But pretty soon, one way or another, we're all standin'.

CHAPTER TWELVE

B
E
R
N
A
R
D

"MAX, HELP ME! HELP ME, MAX!"

I apologize for sounding so needy, but those are just the words a person should yell when they're falling down a giant waterfall along side their ex-roomie who happens to be named, Max.

"Hang on," he shouted, "this will be fun!"

Which is exactly the thing you don't expect to hear when falling down a giant waterfall beside your ex—

We hit the water pretty hard and went under. The good news was we'd stopped falling. The bad news was I was back to my old habit of drowning. The pounding current flipped us over and over like a pair of socks in a dryer. It was pretty confusing. Every time I tried kicking my way back to the surface, someone had moved it. Once in a while, I saw Max shoot past. But instead of panicking, he was laughing which, I don't want to be negative, wasn't too smart, considering how closely laughing is connected to breathing.

On his third or fourth pass I managed to grab hold of him and, trying to be helpful, I shouted into his face, "Breathe! Stop laughing and find some air to breathe!"

He laughed all the harder.

"What you're doing is not possible!" I shouted. "You have to breathe!"

He grinned, tumbled a few more times, and swam back to me laughing so hard he could barely catch his breath, which, let's face it, had been my point all along.

He motioned for me to give it a try. Of course I was still preoccupied with the whole trying-not-to-drown thing, which was looking less and less likely since my lungs were screaming for air and the edges of my vision were already going white.

It was time to get serious. No more fooling around. I had to share what I'd learned from Mrs. Hagen in fourth grade so many years before. I pounded my chest and shouted, "Mammal!" Then, shaking my head at him I shouted, "Not fish."

Max grinned and pushed off, doing enough back flips to make an Olympic gymnast jealous.

My heart broke. There was no way I could make him see reason, so I resumed fighting my way back to the surface . . . only to discover they had replaced it with some very hard river bottom. Before I could turn around, Max arrived and punched me in the stomach. Not hard, just enough to make me gasp – which meant opening my mouth and breathing. And, as hard as this may be to believe, (which it really isn't because as you've probably guessed by now, it's just another one of my weird dreams) I didn't gag, choke, or do any of the usual drowning things. Instead, I breathed in the water as easily as if I were a fish. Amazing.

And Max? He just laughed and did a somersault or two, motioning me to join him. But, of course I was too busy holding my breath. I figured I was just lucky the first time and didn't want to press my luck.

He kept motioning and I kept shaking my head. Fool me once, shame on you. Fool me twice and I drown.

He slugged me again, which meant I gasped again, which meant I breathed again. Then he grabbed my arm and pulled me deeper into the falls, under the pounding water. We tumbled and back-flipped and before I knew it I was laughing, too. I was breathing in water like it was air. Eventually we bobbed back to the surface, still laughing, and I switched back to breathing air as easily as I'd breathed the water.

I sputtered, "How did you . . . how did we—"

"Amphibians," Max said as he started swimming towards shore.

I tried to join him. But since my swimming skills hadn't exactly improved I was under the water as much as on top. But it didn't matter. I could breathe either way.

"What do you mean?" I shouted between dunks. "Amphib . . . ians?"

"We belong to two worlds now," he said. "And we can live in one or the other."

"Or both," I said, blowing out a lung full of water then laughing.

"That's right." He rolled onto his back and floated, waiting for me to catch up.

When I did, I asked, "Now what?"

"Shouldn't this be enough?" he said.

He had a point and, of course, I felt bad until he burst out laughing.

"What?" I said.

"There's never enough. Not when we're talking about an infinite Father who has infinite love."

"But—"

"We're the ones who put up the limits, Bernie, not Him."

I wanted to argue, but he was too busy making sense. After a few more dunks, we finally reached the shore and I started climbing out.

"So where are we now?" I asked.

"The other side."

"Of what?"

"Of where most people are afraid to go."

I turned to him as clueless as ever.

"Look at that sunrise over there, Bernie. Have you ever seen any thing more beautiful?"

I looked and, of course, he was right. The jade green hills in front of us were practically glowing. The same with the mountains beyond, which were all purple and pink. Past them the sky was such a bright red it looked like it was on fire.

I turned back to him and asked, "What do you mean when you said, 'Most are afraid to go?'"

He motioned to the shore and the hills beyond. "This is ours. Every inch of it."

"Are you serious?"

"Trashman paid for all of it."

"Trashman?"

He nodded. "But most of us are too afraid to take it. We stay huddled at the other side. We make all sorts of excuses as to why we're not worthy to cross over. On the surface it all sounds pious and humble, but underneath it's nothing but false humility. A great, deceiving lie."

"'Lie?'"

"The truth is, most of us deny Trashman's greatness. We strip away his glory by refusing to believe he paid enough to get us here. So, in false humility, we live the lie. We never cross over and take the land he intended for us to have . . . until we're dead."

I swallowed. "Dead? I thought this was just a dream. Are you telling me we're dead?"

"No." He chuckled. "Not that type of death. But it's true, you are dead . . . and you've come back to life. And this is the land he promised us. Come on!" He started up the bank and I followed.

"But what about Trashman?" I asked.

"What about him?"

"I don't see him." I turned toward the opposite bank. "Is he still over there?"

Max grinned that grin of his. "No. He's up ahead, waiting."

"Waiting? For what?"

"Not what, Bernie. Who. He's waiting for you."

CHAPTER THIRTEEN

S
A
F
F
R
O
N

It's mornin' and the sun's jus' coming up. I'm sittin' on a curb of some vacant lot near camp watchin' Dough Face across the street. He's pumpin' his arms up and down like some old, white man tryin' to dance. 'Cept he's got a stick in one hand and is wavin' it all round like a fly swatter. I got no idea what's goin' on in the fool's brain and I don't want to know. My brain's busy enough as is.

We been goin' to O.R.B. most every night now. And every time I hear the Reverend speak, I'm more positive than ever . . . I can do it.

I can change. I can stop bein' a low life victim and

75

start controllin' my destiny. All I got to do, is do it. Sure, it's hard. "Hard as nails," he says. But I done harder. And there ain't nobody gonna do it for me. So no more self-pity. No more hand outs. God helps them who helps themselves and I'm diggin' in.

I been tryin' to 'splain it all to Brandylin and Mariposa, but they don't buy it. "The '*man*' he keeps us down," they say, "he's always gonna keep us down." But they'll see. So will JJ. He's been 'cross town last few days doin' business, which is okay. Gives me a chance to clear my head, change my thinkin'. Meantime, I been cleanin' up the camp and workin' real hard at my language. Ain't no time like the present for bein' the new an improved me.

"Are you alright?"

I give a jump and cuss 'til I see it's Max. Guess I got a ways to go. "Sorry," I say.

He just smiles. "You're up early."

"Lots to do. What 'bout you? Ain't seen much of you these last couple days."

"I've been spending some time alone. Trying to be still so I can hear God."

"Yeah? An' what's He sayin'?"

"Not much, I'm afraid. He's been very quiet."

"You oughta come to the O.R.B. meetings. He's sayin' lots there."

He nods and glances away. That's when I see the sadness in his eyes.

"I wouldn't worry," I say. "'Bout hearing God. Probably got lots on His mind, runnin' the universe and all."

He gives another nod then motions to the curb. "May I?"

"Free country." I sound cool and controlled, but

inside I'm excited as some kid. So much I wanna tell him. How I'm feelin' cleaner, lighter. But everything I think to say sounds all stupid and cliché. 'Sides, like the Reverend says, if you're gonna do it, just do it. He'll see.

So, we keep sittin' there 'fore nearly a minute watchin' Dough Face make a fool of himself. Finally, Max says, "Incredible, isn't he?"

"More like moronic."

He smiles.

"What you think he's doin'?" I ask.

"Hard to say. Looks like he might be directing the sunrise."

I turn to him. "What?"

Max grins and nods over to him. I turn back and watch and pretty soon I start seein' it. Well, seein' somethin'. There's a kind of rhythm to the way he's pumpin' them arms. I guess he could be keepin' time. And that stick in his hand? Alright, I s'pose it could be a baton.

I shake my head. "You ask me, he's lost it. What little he had."

"Shh," Max says. "Listen."

I keep watchin' and listenin'. Maybe it's my 'magination, but pretty soon I start seein' stuff – like him motionin' to the paper bag rustlin' past him. Or the cryin' baby from the nearby tenement who gets louder when he raises his hands and softer when he lowers 'em. Or the truck over on the freeway that belches when he points at it.

"Is that . . ." I turn to Max. "Is he doin' that?"

Max just smiles.

We keep sittin' there in the silence, watchin' and listenin'. For a second I think I hear that flute again.

Real faint. The same time I catch a flicker over our heads and look up to see some impossible big bird fillin' the sky. I blink and then it's gone. Probably never was. But the music stays. Faint and airy, like I heard the night the hospital burned down. And that other time over at the landfill.

"You hear that?" I say.

"What?"

"That music."

He closes his eyes and listens.

I cock my head to hear better. "It's like wind, but more. You don't hear that?"

He smiles, then shakes his head kinda sad. "No. Not any more."

"But you and the others, I heard you talk about it. A flute or somethin'."

"That's good. It's good that you hear it."

"Why?"

"It means . . ." he looks to me, "you've been chosen."

"Don't start up again with that royalty bullsh-'" I catch myself.

He tries not to grin.

"Don't start up with that stuff again."

"What I mean," he says, "is that it's good you have the ears to hear."

"Ears to hear what?"

"Well, well, well," we hear JJ aproachin' from behind. "What's the idiot child up to now?"

We turn to see him comin' with a big box of somethin' under his arm.

"Directin' the sunrise," I say. "Can't you tell?"

He shakes his head and cusses.

"What you got in the box?"

He flashes a mischievous grin. "You're gonna like this."

He arrives and opens the lid. He pulls out one of a hundred little necklaces with a funny lookin' charm hangin' from it.

"What's that," I say, motionin' to the charm, "a basket?"

"Ain't no basket," he scoffs. "See them little wheels on the bottom? The little handle on top?"

"Yeah," I say, still not gettin' it.

"It's a shoppin' cart, babe."

"A shoppin' cart?" I look to Max who's as clueless as me.

"People gonna wear 'em." He hands it to me. "All over the city. All over the state, they gonna wear 'em."

I give it a hard look.

"See? It's got them little wire mesh sides an' everything."

I see it now. I ain't impressed, but I see it.

"What you think?"

I glance to Max, but he's turned and is lookin' off and away. I ain't clueless now, just embarrassed. I motion to Doughface. "I think you as crazy as him."

JJ laughs. "We gonna sell, 'em, girl. We gonna sell 'em to every one, every where. And we gonna make tons a money. Trust me, there's big money here. *Real* big."

CHAPTER FOURTEEN

B
E
R
N
A
R
D

"'God is jealous, and the Lord revengeth; the Lord revengeth and is furious; the Lord will take vengeance on his adversaries, and he reserveth wrath for His enemies.'"11

The Reverend strode back and forth in front of the crowd which keeps getting bigger every time we meet. We're all jammed in nice and tight with folks who, I don't want to complain, didn't always have the most perfect personal hygiene habits . . . or imperfect ones, either. Saffron said we were growing so fast because people had videoed Max on their phones the first time he was here and if it was good enough for Maxwell Portenelli everyone figured it was good enough for them.

I was really getting to miss him. Between his going off to talk to God and our supporting the ministry by selling the burning lists and shopping cart necklaces . . . well, I barely got to see him. Of course, it would have been nice if he went to O.R.B. like the rest of us, but the fact that he only went once and hated it, kind of created a problem.

"'But who can endure the day of His coming? Who can stand when He appears? For He will be like a refiner's fire or a launderer's soap.'"[12]

The Reverend had really worked himself up which meant we were really worked up. It was neat to see how everyone was paying attention and, more importantly, how we'd all been changing . . . me, Joey, Nelson, Winona, Ralphy. Even Darcy was showing progress by bringing her snarls down to lip curling sneers. Of course Chloe didn't need changing, since it's pretty hard to improve on perfection. And Saffron? She'd been working real hard on her potty mouth, though none of us could really tell the difference, but at least she was feeling guilty about it, which was the important thing.

The others, like JJ, Brandylin, and Mariposa hadn't come around yet, but we were all working on them and we knew they would. I just wish I could say the same about Max. The Reverend was teaching us so many important things and Max was missing so many of them. It seemed no matter what I said or how I pleaded, he wouldn't change his mind.

Last night was the perfect example. We were all sitting around the fire on our crates, eating Mariposa's culinary masterpiece of pea, radish and Spam stew — peas, courtesy of some cans Darcy borrowed from a nearby grocery store, radishes from a nearby dumpster, and Spam, the only thing a local supermarket couldn't give away during their going out of business sale.

"I still don't understand why you won't go," I said for the hundredth time, which was okay because nobody pays attention to me, anyway – well, except for Max which explains why he answered for the hundredth time:

"The Reverend is a good man but religious philosophy doesn't interest me."

"Why not?" I said.

"Because you and I are not following a religious philosophy, we're living in the midst of a relationship."

Ralphy, who was working on a particularly rubbery radish, said, "But we are still a religion, are we not?"

Max shook his head. "Religion tries to please God by doing good. That's not what God wants."

"Doing good is wrong?" I said.

"No, it's good. But He wants to do it. He wants to live inside us to do it."

"So what is our responsibility?" Ralphy asked. "What do we do?"

"Love Him. Adore Him. He wants to do the heavy lifting. All we have to do is love Him and let Him."

Everyone just kind of stared. I looked down at my bowl as some floating peas began forming a letter on the left side. It was kind of squiggly but you could pretty much tell it was the letter, 'S'.

"Well, whatever the Reverend is teaching is definitely working," Joey said. He motioned to Saffron and rest of the group. "Look how we've all been growing and behaving ourselves."

Max shook his head. "Behavior is not the key."

"Sorry?"

"God is not about behavior modification."

"What's He about, then?" Saffron asked from her rocker.

"Changing hearts."

Two more letters were forming in the center of my bowl, real close, but you could still see they were an 'e' and another 'e.'

Max continued. "Focusing on what we do outside, ignores what Trashman did on the inside."

"I do not understand," Ralphy said. "If the results are the same–"

"But they're not. One is a supernatural win/win: Our old life died with Trashman . . . God's new life grows inside us. The other is a man-made lose/lose: Trashman's sacrifice is theory . . . our 'goodness' grows from our own prideful efforts."

Now, everyone was looking at him.

He continued. "If I'm understanding this correctly, the old life will do anything to stay alive . . . even become religious."

I glanced down to see the last letter forming in the right of my bowl. It was one of the same letters I kept seeing when playing Freeway Scrabble – the letter 'D.' I looked up, wanting to share my discovery, but everybody was too busy thinking. Actually, them being busy was a good thing because that meant I could secretly dump the stew on the ground without being noticed. And that was a good thing because it would probably kill off some of the rats that had been paying us late night visits.

"But we can't jus' sit here on our–" Saffron searched for a "G-rated" word but failed. "I mean He expects us to do somethin'."

Max nodded. "Yes. He wants us to adore Him. To saturate ourselves in His love."

The Reverend slapped the safe hard and it brought me back to his talk. "'Great is the wrath of the Lord that is kindled against us, because our fathers have not hearkened unto the words of this book, to do according unto all that which is written concerning us.'" [13]

He continued pacing. "For those who choose to ignore His word and follow our anti-God government, know this . . . God will not be mocked. The day of judgment is upon us. A sign shall soon appear. Tonight, tomorrow, the day after – it shall soon appear. God's holy wrath shall be unleashed upon our enemies. And we shall be free. Once and for all, we shall be free!"

Lots of folks shouted and clapped. Me, too. But even then, it kind of made me sad, wishing Max was there. It sure would have cheered him up. I'm serious. Because lately, he'd been coming back from his times with God pretty depressed. That's why earlier this morning, as me, Max, Nelson and Chloe were sitting around drinking the coffee Chloe had made, I flat out asked him why he was so sad. Friends can be honest like that. At first he didn't say much. But when I kept asking, which like I said is one of my specialties, he finally answered.

"I'm afraid He's not saying very much to me right now."

"God?" I asked, crunching away on some coffee grounds.

He nodded. "He hasn't said a word."

"Why?"

"I'm not sure. I've got some ideas, but I'm not sure."

Chloe quietly cleared her voice like she was going

to say something. We all turned to her. Finally she spoke. "Maybe . . . maybe He's not talking to you because He's mad at you."

Max kind of frowned. "Mad at me for . . .?"

She shrugged. "For not going to the meetings."

"Is that what He told you?"

She shook her head and looked down.

"I'm sorry," he said. "If God told you that, then I should–"

She shook her head again and I explained. "Chloe's trying not to pay attention to that stuff anymore."

"Stuff?" He turned back to her. "You mean your gift?"

She kept looking down.

I answered. "The Reverend says we have all the words we ever need from God – locked up, nice and secure inside his safe."

"He said that?" Max asked.

I nodded. "He says God has said all He's ever going to say."

"But . . ." Max frowned. "How do you love someone if they never talk to you?"

I started to give my answer then realized I didn't have one to give, so I just sat there chewing my coffee.

Finally, Chloe said, "We have His letters."

"That's right," I agreed, "We have the Ancient Text."

Max thought a moment then he took a deep, long breath and asked, "Have you ever wondered why the Reverend keeps the Ancient Text locked up in that safe?"

Luckily, the Reverend had told us just the other

night. Even more luckily, I remembered. "He keeps it locked up so it's protected from the people."

Max nodded. "Maybe . . . Or maybe he's protecting the people from it."

"What do you mean?" I said. "What would he protect the people from?"

"God."

It was my turn to frown.

"Bernie, how many times have we heard of God saying crazy, unpredictable things?"

"Lots," I said.

"Exactly. But if people try to lock up those sayings and control them, His very words can do harm."

I stole a look to Chloe, who kept staring at her floating coffee grounds.

He continued. "His word is like some, giant, two-edged sword. If God is free to use His words His way, they can do incredible, life-giving things. But if they are locked up and controlled by men, they can enslave and hurt, even kill."

For the first time Nelson spoke. "'The Letter kills but the Spirit gives life.'"[14]

Max nodded. "That's right. If God's word is energized by His Spirit, it gives life. But if it's locked up and controlled by man . . . it can imprison and kill."

I didn't understand him then, and I don't understand him now. But I did understand the Reverend when he pounded on the safe and shouted, "'For the wages of sin is death!'"[15] "Do you want to die?"

"No!" we shouted.

"Do you want this great country of ours to die?"

"No!"

"Then come join with me and live. Let us come together and put an end to our sins! And let us extinguish the sins of our great country!"

We all broke into cheers. Like I said, I didn't understand everything Max said. But I understood the Reverend. And as I looked around the room, it was pretty clear everyone else did, too.

CHAPTER FIFTEEN

D
R

A
A
D
I
L

"Father? Can you hear me?"

"Maxwell? Mr. Portenelli?"

Alexis turned to me – giant sunglasses, baggy sweatshirt, jeans torn at all the correct places to warrant a $350.00 price tag. "You sure you have the right alley?" she called.

I nodded. "Nineteen hundred Block. They're sure it's somewhere here."

The 'it' was where they suspected Maxwell to be holding his nightly meetings. The 'they' was the Mayor and his office. Nearly a week ago witnesses had reported Maxwell and his group entering this alley and disappearing. And each successive evening more street people were showing up and performing similar disappearing acts.

"Father, are you here?"

Did I feel bad, giving into the Mayor and using the daughter as bait? Of course. But not as bad as avoiding picking up bars of soap in some prison shower for the next twenty years. With the help of Johnny Walker, I'd spent hours mulling over the decision. When it was reached, I returned to the Mayor's office with what I felt to be the perfect compromise. I'd do whatever he wanted whenever he wanted it. With just one exception. Alexis and I would be the only ones to flush out her father. No police. It would be a simple and heartfelt father/daughter reunion . . . with his friendly doctor nearby to convince him to return to treatment. The syringe of Propofol I carried would only be used to seal the deal.

"Father?"

I had a difficult time reading the daughter. There was obviously no love loss between them, but as she kept calling, I sensed a vulnerability, almost urgency. I'd seen it in the hospital when she spoke to him and it was even stronger out here.

We'd put in nearly an hour before I heard the scraping of metal against concrete.

"There!" she shouted. "What's that?"

I turned to see a steel door crack open.

"Dr. Aadil?" a familiar voice called. It was followed by a head with shower cap and swim goggles.

"Raphael?"

"What are you doing here?" He leaned further out to check the alley.

"We've come looking for you." I approached, motioning for Alexis to join me. "This is Maxwell's daughter."

We arrived and, always the gentlemen, Raphael opened the door wider, bowed his head and reached for her hand. She looked at me in concern. I nodded and she reluctantly let him take it.

"Señorita," he said, gently kissing it, "it is my sincerest pleasure to meet you."

"Thank–" she cleared her voice. "Thank you."

Suddenly, I heard scuffing feet behind us. I turned to see two, four, five SWAT members materialize from the shadows and storm toward us.

"What are you doing?" I shouted. "This is not what we agree–"

Raphael tried ducking inside but he was too late. One of the officers grabbed the door, another grabbed him. But that didn't stop him from being a hero.

"Stand aside!" he yelled as they pulled him out into the alley. "Raphael Montoya Hernandez III–"

"What's happening?" Alexis cried as they shoved her onto the pavement.

"–has given you fair warning!" The little man continued shouting as they dragged him off. "Do not force me to use my super powers!"

I tried to block the others from entering. "Our agreement said nothing about–"

They slammed me hard against a brick wall just inside and I saw stars. They ran past me and down a stairwell. The yelling and screaming began. I turned and stumbled down the steps after them. Amidst the yellow glow of candlelight, I saw the officers pushing their way through the tightly packed crowd, swinging batons at any who had the misfortune of being in the way.

"Maxwell Portenelli!" they shouted. "We're looking for Maxwell Portenelli!"

The people outnumbered the police twenty to one but like frightened sheep, they screamed and cried, trying to duck and dodge the blows.

Another voice rose up. Amplified. Full of authority:

"*'Be strong and courageous!'*" It came from the speakers at the front of the room. "'*Do not be afraid for the Lord your God goes with you! Be strong and courageous!'*" it repeated. "*The Lord God goes with you! Be strong and courageous! Be strong and courageous!'*" [16]

It seemed to inspire and give the people strength.

"Do not be afraid for the Lord is with you!"

And the more it shouted, the stronger they grew.

"*For the great day of His wrath is come; and who shall be able to stand?*"[17] *Be strong and courageous. Do not tremble or be afraid!'*"

With the growing strength they began to resist. They pushed back – grabbing batons, the officers' arms, leaping onto their backs. Those who were knocked to the floor clung to the officer's legs, bringing them down where others began to kick at whatever they could reach.

"Dr. Aadil!" someone shouted. "Doctor!"

I spun around to see Bernard being shoved and jostled. Blood streamed down his face.

"What are you doing here?" he yelled.

"I–"

A baton slammed into my right shoulder. The pain was immediate and sharp. I turned to see the officer raising it for a second blow, when suddenly a giant, homeless man broadsided him.

"*'And my wrath shall wax hot,*" the voice shouted.

"And I will kill you with the sword-"[18]

Two women joined the homeless man and jumped onto the officer's back. He staggered, swinging his club, but they hung on. He turned, stumbled, then fell to the floor, where the merciless kicking began.

"Did you bring them?" A woman's voice shouted.

I turned to see Winona, pointing her mascara container at me with both hands like it was a miniature light saber.

"No," I shouted. "I mean, yes. I'm not sure–"

Something struck the back of my head. The stars returned. I felt my knees buckle but managed to turn and see Darcy Hamilton. She was breathing hard and holding a folding chair like a baseball bat. I tried speaking but that part of my brain had already ceased functioning. She swung the chair again, this time hitting my face, throwing me backwards, sound and light spinning, then fading to nothing.

CHAPTER SIXTEEN

A
L
E
X
I
S

"How many times do I have to tell you? Once your Nazi Storm Troopers threw me on the ground and ran over me I didn't see a single thing."

Some Lieutenant, complete with outdated slacks and a pathetic excuse for a sports coat, paced in front of my gray, metal table. "And you never followed them inside?"

I motioned to my bandaged forehead. "They made it clear they didn't need my help."

Sergeant Good-Cop, with the figure of a Macy Day Parade balloon, stood in the opposite corner and chuckled, "Looks like they could have used it."

The Lieutenant shot him a look. But it was true. By the time the crowd had finished with the city's finest, there wasn't a one of them left standing.

"And when the people left the cellar?" he asked. "How were they?"

My phone on the table vibrated for the hundredth time. I hoped it was Troy back at the apartment wanting some R and R. But I knew it was the kiddies at the studio wanting some help. We had four weeks before New York. I was only behind by seven.

He repeated, "Ms. Portenelli? Tell me about the people who left the cellar."

I shrugged. "Some were pretty beat up. Others weren't. But they all helped each other to get out."

"And your father?"

"I never saw him. He wasn't at the meeting."

"And Dr. Addil?"

"I have no idea. When your goons finally dragged themselves away, he wasn't with them."

"And no one in the crowd told you where they were going?"

"They didn't exactly trust me."

"Surely you heard someone say something about where they–"

The door flew open, banging into the wall. And there stood Robert, come to my rescue. He wore a lavender, silk suit with pink tie and white loafers. In his hand he carried my Teacup Maltese who, in his excitement to see me, began nonstop yapping . . . and peeing like a racehorse.

Toulouse!" I cried.

The Lieutenant jumped back, unsuccessful at avoiding the stream. "Who are you? How did–"

"I am her brother."

"Get out!" he shouted, brushing the urine off his jacket. "You have no right–"

"I have every right. And as soon as our lawyers get here– Oh, sweetie," he'd spotted my forehead and swept toward me, "are you okay?"

"I'll be fine now," I said, taking Toulouse into my arms.

"Now don't be a martyr." Robert played the faux gay card to the max as he pulled up a chair. "Let me see."

"Get him out of here!" the Lieutenant bellowed.

Robert pushed back my hair. "Oh, that's terrible! Awful. It should be worth a minimum of fifty thousand, don't you think?"

I turned my head, pretending to wince. "Not to mention this neck injury I just noticed."

"Oh, Sweetie."

"And all this mental anguish."

"I see a Lexus Sports Coup in your future.

"I was hoping for a Lamborghini.

"I'm sure we can get both . . . unless, of course, the strapping Lieutenant here decides to release you now."

The strapping Lieutenant caught our drift and was furious. Before he could react, another fashion disaster, this one with a jelly belly, barged in. He crossed to the TV in the corner and snapped it on. "You'll want to see this," was all he said.

"Would anyone mind if I continued this interview!" the Lieutenant shouted.

Up on the screen, a distinguished black dude with a beard and three-piece suit was speaking directly at us through his cell phone. "We did not start this war," he said, "but I swear to you with the help of God,

Almighty, we shall end it."

The picture cut to another cell phone image. This one showing a mass of people screaming and getting their heads bashed in by my SWAT pals. A woman raised her arm to protect her bloodied face but was struck. She dropped to her knees and was hit again. Other images followed – flying clubs, beaten and screaming victims.

The man's voice continued:

"The great and terrible day of the Lord hath arrived. Word has gone forth to our brothers and sisters across the land who, at this very moment, are answering God's call to come join us."

The picture switched and I gasped. It was my father – scraggy beard, flyaway hair, totally oblivious to his wardrobe. He was talking to another group of street people.

"Already, the great heroes of faith are joining the movement."

I felt my throat tighten. I wanted to look away, but couldn't.

The picture changed again – this time to someone in a dark, dingy room. Even in the bad light you could clearly see it was Dr. Aadil. He sat on a small bed, dazed and disheveled. There was a gash on his right cheek that rivaled the one on my forehead. He was squinting up at the camera, listening to a question someone off screen was asking, as the narrator continued:

"Already, we are taking prisoners of war."

"My name?" the doctor said. "Aadil. Dr. Timothy Aadil."

"Occupation?" the off screen voice asked.

"What?"

"Who do you work for?"

"The Department of Religious Affairs."

The picture changed and the narrator reappeared. "The time has come. God will no longer be mocked. Those who believe will join us. Those who refuse will face His fiery judgment. I urge you my friends, choose this day who you will serve. Examine your wicked hearts. Because those not fighting for us will be fighting against us. And not just us. They will be fighting against God, almighty. For He is our strength. He is our helper. And He will bless each and every one who rises to meet the call. God bless each of us. And God bless America."

The picture switched to a TV studio where some self-appointed expert trapped in a bad suit, began repeating everything we'd just seen. But I barely heard. My mind was reeling, trying to understand what I'd seen and was feeling.

CHAPTER SEVENTEEN

S
A
F
F
R
O
N

"Stay back," I said.

"But—"

"Stay back. I'll tell you when it's safe."

Max agreed. I looked 'round the corner again. A couple cops was comin' down the street. One of 'em spots me sneakin' a peek, which probably looks suspicious, so he shouts. "You there?" He breaks from his partner and starts toward me. No surprise. For the past couple days they been shakin' down everyone on the street they think is O.R.B. which is gettin' to be quite a lot.

"What's going on?" Max whispers behind me.

Instead of answerin' I step out, flippin my hair back all seductive like, and say to the cop. "You talkin' to me?"

He keeps comin' forward. My heart's poundin' but I keep playin' the part. I lean against the wall, leg propped up, making sure he sees plenty of thigh.

It does the trick. He comes to a stop and says, "You see any groups in the area, any unlawful assembly?"

"I ain't seen nothin' unlawful," I says, "but you can." I touch my thigh. "All you want."

He shakes his head and swears, turnin' to join his partner.

"And your friend, too, if you like?"

They ignore me and keep headin' down the street. When they're far enough away I tell Max, "It's clear, let's go." He steps out and we 'bout to cross when the cop turns back 'roud and I whisper to Max, "Grab me."

"What?"

I take his arm and wrap it round my hips. "Hold me tight like we doin' business."

He tries pullin' away. "I'm sorry, I—"

"Do it!"

He does, so embarrassed and awkward, I have to keep holdin' his arm in place. Funny, two weeks ago I'd be arrested for solicitatin'. Now I gotta pretend to do it so I don't get arrested.

But that ain't the only change that's happenin'. Like I said, O.R.B's growin' by leaps and bounds. Folks are comin' in from around the state. So far there ain't been much violence, least from our side. But the police are gearin' up and everyone's lockin' down. Everyone knows a real war's 'bout to begin.

And, like any war, you sometimes gotta cut your losses. That's what happened to me an JJ. It came after last night's meetin'. Because of the crackdown and its growin' size, O.R.B. don't meet in one place no more. 'Stead we're scattered 'bout the whole city, gatherin' round somebody's cell phone or computer listenin' to the Reverend's nightly talks.

And one of those times JJ shows up, high and wantin' some sugar. And that's when I tell him things has got to change. I got to be holy now like God is holy. More than that. Me and him gotta start bein' equally yoked. If we stay together, He's gotta join the group and start listen' to the Reverend.

'Course JJ hits the ceiling. "What you talkin' 'bout?" he shouts. "I burn my lists like everyone else."

"It's more than that," I say. "You gotta show the fruits of your ways."

"An' do what? Join yer little suicide group?"

"It ain't so little no more. Look 'round you, JJ. It's a whole movement, now."

"It's still suicide."

"Not if God's in it."

He stares at me, mouth hangin' open. "You really serious."

"It's the most serious I ever been."

"So you and me, no more goodies, 'til I start listenin' to the Reverend an goin' to your meetin's."

"You can stand in a garage all day long and say yer a Mercedes. But if you ain't behavin' like a Mercedes you ain't no Mercedes."

He shakes his head and swears.

"And we ain't doin' no more a that either."

"You crazy, woman!" he yells. "You all crazy!"

"You know where the door is," I say. "No one's askin' you to stay."

And he don't. Ten minutes later he got his stuff packed and is gone. It makes me sad, havin' so much history together and everythin'. Don't get me wrong, we had lots a fights and lots a times he left, but he always come back. This time though, I don't think so. And I shouldn't care. Cause like the Reverend says, "Yer either with God or yer against Him."

And I ain't the only one feelin' that. Lots of Max's group are, too. Especially Butch Babe with the tattoos. (Darcy, they call her). She's been listenin' real careful to the Reverend and the two of us, we been workin' real hard and havin' some real good talks.

Wish I could say the same for Max. In some ways he's worse than JJ. The man just won't budge. No matter what we say, no matter how we try to make him listen, he don't agree. That's why we was happy and surprised when he accepted the Reverend's invitation for us to meet with him for a "private session." Talk 'bout an honor. Darcy says she thinks it's gonna be like an intervention thing and she's probably right. I hope so. Course, with the police and everybody on alert, we can't all go at once. We gotta travel separately so we ain't followed. But the point is, we're all goin'.

Except for Mariposa who because of his obvious sins, left us over a week ago.

And my lovely Brandylin.

How she broke my heart. Word was she'd been sleepin' with some guy. Course I don't believe it 'til me and Darcy come back from dumpster divin' and catch 'em in an abandoned car goin at it like dogs in heat. The kid, some late twenties tweaker, is no problem. Me and Darcy had him out of the car and down on the pavement kickin' the crap out of him in seconds.

But Brandylin. All the time we was cleanin' his

clock, she's yellin' and screamin'. "Momma, stop. Momma! Momma!"

Course, we got no intention a stoppin' til he finally drug his sorry butt out of our sight along with plenty a threats from us about ending his reproduction abilities if we ever catch him again.

"Momma, what'd you do?" she yells.

"What'd I do? What'd you do?"

"He's a nice boy."

"He's a grown man!"

"I was just showin' my appreciation."

My eyes flare. "'Preciation for what?" I grab her arm. She don't answer so I grab the other, makin her face me. "What's he got that makes you think you gotta show 'preciation? Brandylin?" I shake her. "Answer me!"

"A little blow, alright!"

I stare at her. I can't find my voice.

"And some crank, but not a lot." She looks up at me, chin out, all defiant.

"You're havin' sex with that man for drugs? How long?"

"Not long."

"How long!"

"What do you care?"

"What do I care?" My voice is shakin'. "My kid's sellin' her body for drugs like some, some . . ."

"Go ahead, say it!"

I can't, so she does. "Whore?"

My heart's hammerin' in my chest.

"A whore, is that what I am, Momma?"

I can't breathe.

"So I guess we're no different, are we? Like mother like daughter!"

I slap her hard.

But she turns right back at me, eyes watering. "I'm fourteen, Momma. It's my body an' I'll do what I want."

My mind's spinnin' with a thousand things.

"And I'm sorry if that makes your God mad. I'm sorry if you think I'm goin' to hell."

"I never—"

"You don't have to. I see it. Every day when you look at me, at JJ. And poor Mariposa, who knows where she is now. But I ain't never followin' this God of yours, Momma. I'm gonna have a real life. I'm gonna do the drugs I want, have the sex I want. I'm gonna have fun. You hear me? And if that makes your God all pissy, then tough. Cause from what I seen, I'd rather go to hell where he ain't than be in a heaven where he is."

"You don't mean that."

"Just watch me."

She yanks her arm free then spins around and starts off.

'Course I call after her. "Brandylin . . ."

But she just keeps walkin'. Her back's to me, but the way her body shakes and her hands up at her face I know she's cryin'.

"Brandylin!"

But she just keeps walkin' 'til she turns the corner and disappears from sight.

That was four nights ago. I ain't heard from her since.

CHAPTER EIGHTEEN

B
E
R
N
A
R
D

It was pretty exciting getting to spend personal time with the Reverend, given his busy schedule of running a revolution and all. And it was the first time in a long time that the whole gang was together – even Dr. Aadil, though we could only wave at him before they closed and locked his bedroom door. Still, except for the big gash on his cheek, he looked pretty good for a man going to hell.

Like I said before, everybody was getting better. Winona was barely a germaphobe anymore. Ralphy disposed of his cape and goggles and only wore his shower cap (in case a third of the stars fell from Heaven). Darcy channeled her anger more constructively by burning off patches of her tattoos every night. Even Joey didn't hang on to the edge of chairs anymore (though he always carried an extra belt to strap in should the rapture go haywire). And finally there was Nelson who, although he didn't change, was a lot more agreeable than he used to be.

The Reverend had moved O.R.B's headquarters to an apartment in the Tenderloin. It was a lot higher up than the cellar, but a lot more run down. He greeted us with a big smile, ushered us in and offered Max a seat across from him at a beat-up kitchen table. The rest of us sat on a sagging sofa and matching loveseat, except for Chloe who stood off to the side kinda sad. She never blurted out embarrassing stuff anymore which was a good thing, but I could tell she felt guilty for thinking them. I tried to make her feel better by standing up and joining her. I even took her hand. Don't get me wrong, I'm not a perv or anything. I mean it'll never go any farther than hand holding, until we get married, and only then after we have a child or two. But for today I thought she needed it.

I leaned over and whispered, "Is everything all right?"

"How should I know?" she said. She shook her bangs over her eyes. "Stop asking. I don't know anything." (Which I knew was a lie but at least it was a good start).

Once everyone was settled, the Reverend took his seat and said to Max. "I've so looked forward to our meeting."

Max nodded politely. "Thank you."

"Your friends here tell me you are having trouble with some of God's Ancient Text."

"No. Actually, I believe it's all true."

"Oh. Well that's excellent news."

I breathed a sigh of relief. Things were going to be good after all.

"It's manipulating the Ancient Text to fit your own private agenda that I find offensive."

Okay, maybe not so good. Everyone got real quiet – except for some children who were singing and playing down at the end of the hall. They weren't loud, but loud enough. Every once in a while I could make out what they were saying – actually only one word of what they were saying, but they kept saying it over and over again:

"*Seed, seed . . . seed . . . seed, seed . . .*"

Nobody else seemed to notice so I tried not to, too. Because, like I said, everybody was getting better – although, I did catch Ralphy sizing up the guard at the door. Not that he didn't have his reasons. The man was huge and scary with huge and scary muscles. When I caught his eye, I gave him a smile, hoping to make friends . . . and let him know I appreciated someone was keeping the steroid companies in business.

He didn't exactly smile back, but he did start to hum. Nice and loud. Again, no one else seemed to hear, well, except for the Reverend's assistant who was smiling. She was a beautiful woman with skin so perfectly smooth and shiny it was like a doll's. As she moved around the room passing out water in paper cups, she began dancing to the guard's humming. Little steps at first. But then they got bigger and bigger. Of course no one else noticed that either, and it might have been easy to ignore, if she didn't keep making all those suggestive movements with her hips and other girly parts.

The Reverend asked if she would bring out the Ancient Text from the next room. She nodded and, still smiling at the guard, twirled and swirled out of the room. When she was gone, the Reverend brought out a pair of surgical gloves like they wear in hospitals. He was putting them on when she danced back in carrying a very large and very old book. Its leather cover was cracked and wrinkled almost as bad as her hands which I hadn't noticed until she set the book on the table. Poor thing. You could tell they'd been in some terrible accident by the way the skin was all crinkles and wrinkles . . . not at all like her smooth, shiny face.

Once his gloves were on, the Reverend turned to Max. "Which part of the Ancient Text do you wish to discuss first?"

"I, uh . . ." Max reached for his water and took a sip. "I'm not sure."

"You're not sure?"

"No, I've never read it before."

The Reverend scowled. "Well that may make our discussion a little difficult."

Max nodded and took another sip. That's when I came to his rescue. "We've got Nelson here," I said. "Nelson knows everything."

The Reverend turned to Nelson who bobbed slightly and quoted, "'An investment in knowledge pays the best interest.'"[19]

The Reverend blinked and stared a moment. Then, turning back to Max he said, "Given the time restraints, I suggest we go directly to the points and discuss the issues upon which we disagree."

"Alright," Max said. "First of all . . ." he took

another sip of water. "God does not expect us to overcome our bad behavior on our own. Or to overcome bad people. Those are His jobs."

"Behavior and people. You're speaking of two separate issues."

"Not really. Whether we fight the man attacking us from the inside or the one attacking us from the out, the battle belongs to God."

"I see. And what exactly do you understand our part to be in this battle?"

"We're to love and adore Him. To put our faith in His power and not our works."

"Hm." The Reverend carefully opened the book and began turning its pages. When he found a spot, he cleared his throat and read. "'But wilt thou know, O vain man, that faith without works is dead?'"[20] He looked up. "That sounds pretty clear to me. I fail to see how I've turned any of that into my own 'private agenda.'" He turned back to the book and repeated, "'Faith without works is dead.'"

Nelson, who like I said, was trying to be a lot more helpful, cocked his head and quoted, "'Even so faith, if it hath not works, is dead, being alone.'"[21]

The Reverend nodded, "My point exactly." He turned and waited for Max's response.

Max stayed quiet for a long moment. There was only the sound of the children playing. I could make out two of their words now:

"Seed . . . Earth. Seed, seed . . . Earth, Earth, Earth . . ."

Max took another sip of water and answered. "I agree with what you've read, but the works have to come from inside. They don't come from me but from God's power working inside me." Max turned to us. "You remember? How Trashman breathed into us?"

I nodded real big, until I noticed everyone looking down, so I changed my nod to kind of small.

Max continued. "You remember the dreams you all had when we first left the hospital? How Trashman breathed into each of you?" He looked at Chloe. "How His breath gave you life?"

She pulled deeper into her sweater. Everyone kept examining the carpet.

Finally Ralphy spoke up. "That was a long time ago."

Joey added. "It was an experience, Max. And experiences are not to be trusted. Not like the Ancient Text." He nodded to the Reverend who nodded back.

After a moment, the Reverend continued, "And this other business . . . that you disagree with destroying God's enemies?"

"God has no enemies," Max said. "Not after Trashman's death."

"I see. Then, perhaps you can explain this passage." The Reverend carefully turned the pages until he found the right place and read. "'Joshua took all these royal cities and their kings and put them to the sword. He totally destroyed them, as Moses the servant of the Lord had commanded.'"[22]

Nelson looked up to the ceiling and quoted, "'Thou shalt smite them, and utterly destroy them.'"[23]

The Reverend read some more. "'For the day of the Lord of hosts shall be upon every one that is proud and lofty, and upon every one that is lifted up; and he shall be brought low.'"[24]

Winona coughed slightly and spoke up. "And that

was my sin." We turned to her. "Pride," she said. "I thought too highly of myself."

"Me, too," Ralphy said.

"And me," Darcy mumbled.

Nelson nodded. "'He mocks proud mockers but gives grace to the humble.'"[25]

Winona turned to Max, not mad or anything, just trying to explain. "Because you kept telling me I was important, I kept getting 'proud and lifted up.' Like I thought I was somebody great, somebody special."

"That's right," Joey said. "Me, too."

"But you are special," Max said. "Each of you is God's favorite child. Remember? You're each a remarkable masterpiece."

The Reverend quickly flipped to another section and read, "'Woe unto you, when all men shall speak well of you! For so did their fathers to the false profits.'" [26]

Nelson finished the quote, "'. . . they boast about themselves and flatter others for their own advantage.'"[27]

The Reverend nodded. "That's the real truth of the matter." He found another place and read: "'Man, who is but a maggot-- a son of man, who is only a worm.'"[28]

I kept looking to Max, waiting for him to say something. Anything. But he didn't. How could he? If he tried, he'd be arguing against God's Ancient Text.

Nelson added, "'We are all as an unclean thing, and all our righteousnesses are like filthy rags.'"[29]

And that was just the beginning. The Reverend and Nelson just kept going at it, on and on, reading and quoting, reading and quoting. It got to the point where I almost felt sorry for Max . . . if it wasn't something he needed to hear so badly.

"'The wicked is reserved to the day of destruction. They shall be brought forth to the day of wrath.'"[30]

"'He will repay, fury to his adversaries, recompence to His enemies.'"[31]

"'Throw them into the fiery furnace, where there will be weeping and gnashing of teeth.'"[32]

And Max? He just sat there, taking it. What else can you do when you've been so wrong and everyone else is so right?

CHAPTER NINETEEN

B
E
R
N
A
R
D

Nelson and the Reverend were both really smart and really impressive. It was like a game to see who would run out of quotes first, and it was a lot of fun to watch. Of course it would have been more fun if it didn't hurt Max so much. Not that he was in pain, at least on the outside. But inside you could tell he was getting pretty beat up. In fact, after a while he just closed his eyes and lowered his head. But you knew he wasn't going to sleep.

Then, sometime around midnight, he started to shake his head. It was just a little at first, but he kept shaking it harder and harder until the Reverend finally had to stop (which I guess made Nelson the winner). Everyone got real quiet. Well except for the kids playing down the hall. Why anyone let them do that this time of night was beyond me. But they just kept playing and singing. Now I could make out three words:

"*Fall. Earth, Earth. Seed, Earth . . . fall. . . . Fall, fall, fall . . .*"

"I'm sorry," the Reverend said to Max. "Did you have a rebuttal?"

Max raised his head and opened his eyes. He looked a lot more tired than before. His voice was faint and raspy, but you could still hear it. "You know everything that's been written about God?"

The Reverend smiled kindly. "Who can know everything?" He tried to be humble, but he couldn't lie, either. "But it is true, I have dedicated my entire life to studying Him."

Max nodded, then answered, "You've studied Him . . . but you don't know Him."

The Reverend scowled. "Pardon me?"

Max said, "I can give you a road map of Paris. I can provide dozens of guidebooks, photographs, DVD's. But if you've never been to Paris . . . you'll never know Paris. You will never experience it."

I had no idea what vacations had to do with what they were talking about, but apparently the Reverend did. "And I understand you go there?" he said. "You claim to visit God?"

Max slowly nodded.

"And have all those lovely talks with Him?"

Max started to nod, then caught himself.

"What?" the Reverend said. "He doesn't talk to you?"

A flicker of sadness crossed Max's face. "Not any more."

It made me sad to see him sad, but he wasn't

through. He raised his hand and tapped his chest. "But I know He's here."

"Where?" the Reverend asked.

"Inside."

The Reverend sighed. "And now, no doubt, you're going to share with us some decades' old, New Age, drivel."

It was Max's turn to frown.

The Reverend quoted, "'I am God . . . we are all God . . . the God within.' Mr. Portenelli, those are nothing but rehashed heresies from the last century."

Max's frown deepened. "But . . . they're in the Ancient Text." He turned to Nelson. "We studied them at the hospital."

Nelson nodded and took a breath. He was about to quote something, when the Reverend cut him off. "They are irrelevant."

"What?" Max asked hoarsely. "Why?"

"As I've explained, they were embraced by New Age heretics nearly a century ago. And, as you may have noticed, none of us here subscribe to such thinking.

Max stared at him a moment like he didn't believe what he was hearing, like he didn't know how to answer. Then he looked down and just shook his head again.

"What?" The Reverend asked.

More head shaking.

"No, please. Enlighten us."

Finally Max said, "If you didn't like that, you're not going to like this."

"What?"

Everyone got real silent again. Well, except for the kids. They'd added another word and it was definitely not one of my favorites. It's the same one I keep seeing over and over again when I play Freeway Scrabble:

"*Die . . . Die, die, die . . .*"

Max reached for his water cup which was empty. You could tell by the way his hand was shaking a little that he was pretty tired.

The Reverend sat waiting.

We all sat waiting.

Finally Max spoke, "Trashman told me . . ." He paused.

"Yes?"

"He told me that He gave us the authority to rule with God. He said we are sitting with God on His throne and learning to rule."

"Did he now?" The Reverend leaned back and relaxed, though you could see the muscles in his jaw tightening.

Max nodded. "Yes."

"I see. But doesn't that sound just a little, oh, I don't know, blasphemous? Besides being delusional, egotistical and completely impossible?"

"Impossible?"

"No one can be in two places at the same time. To be ruling in Heaven at the same time you are here on earth? Ludicrous."

"Actually," Joey said, "that's no longer the case."

Everyone turned to him.

"Newtonian physics as we know it has been proven to be outdated and incorrect. Now, with quantum mechanics, it is very possible, even likely, for an object to occupy multiple locations simultaneously."

"That's absurd."

"That's science." Joey said, pulling his seat belt just a little tighter.

Nelson bobbed and chimed in. "'God raised us up with Christ and seated us with him in the heavenly realms in Christ Jesus.'"[33]

The Reverend turned to Nelson. "You would dare put us at the same level as Christ?"

But the little guy was just warming up:

"'Do you not know that the saints will judge the world? . . . Do you not know that we will judge angels?'"[34]

"Blasphemy!"

"'Now if we are children, then we are heirs – heirs of God and co-heirs with Christ, if indeed we share in his sufferings in order that we may also share in his glory.'"[35]

The Reverend's eyes were getting pretty narrow. "Do you, in your wildest dreams, think you can share God's glory?"

"'I have given them the glory that you gave me, that they may be one as we are one . . .'"[36]

"Satan, be gone!"

The outburst made us all jump. But the Reverend wasn't finished. "That's right, you heard me. Only Satan, himself, would dare make such claims." He turned back to Max. "You say you believe the Word of God?"

Max nodded.

"Then listen carefully, my friend, to the devil's lie when he tempted Eve to eat the forbidden fruit. Without turning to the Ancient Text, he quoted, "'For God doth know that in the day ye eat thereof, then your eyes shall be opened, and ye shall be as gods . . .'"[37] He turned to Nelson. "Have I misquoted anything?"

Nelson shook his head.

"Do you have anything to add?"

Always helpful, Nelson nodded and quoted, "'I am the Lord . . . my glory will I not give to another . . .'"38

The Reverend nodded and quoted, "'Hear, O Israel: The Lord our God is one Lord.'"

Nelson nodded and quoted, "'I am the first, and I am the last; and beside me there is no God.'"40

Then the Reverend. "'See now that I, even I, am he, and there is no god with me . . .'" 41

Then Nelson, "'The Lord he is God in heaven above, and upon the earth beneath: there is none else.'"42

It was getting to be just like old times, each of them out-quoting the other.

"'. . . thou art the God, even thou alone'" 43

And just like old times, Max closed his eyes and slowly lowered his head.

"'Thou shalt have no other gods before me.'"44

"'For thou, Lord, art high above all the earth: thou art exalted far above all gods.'"45

On and on they went. And on some more. With each quote, Max seemed to drop his head a little lower and get a little smaller. I'm not sure how long they went on like that because I finally stopped paying attention. I wasn't trying to be rude. It was just too painful. Max was too good of a friend. And, like I said, they just kept going at him, really beating him up.

I closed my own eyes and focused on the kids down the hall. Why neighbors didn't complain was beyond me. But they just kept on playing and singing:

"*Fall, fall . . . Earth. Die, fall, Earth. Seed . . . seed, seed,*

seed . . ."

Eventually Chloe poked me in the side and I opened my eyes to see the Reverend was standing up. By the looks of things it was finally over. And by the look on Max's face, so was he. I don't want to be rude, but he looked awful, like he'd really been hit hard and beaten up bad, which of course, he really had.

The Reverend carefully removed his gloves and went around the room shaking each of our hands and telling us how much he appreciated what we had done and how much Max would appreciate it, too . . . maybe not now, but some day, soon. He even shook Max's hand and said he hoped there were no hard feelings and that he looked forward to him joining us someday soon. "Because," he gave one last quote, "'He that is not with me is against me.'" [46]

Max may have nodded. I'm not sure. He was too tired to say much or do much, except follow us out the apartment door and into the hallway. The kids who had been playing there had disappeared. Probably gone to bed. No one talked as we reached the stairway and started down the steps. There was nothing left to say. But, of course, that never stopped me.

"Are you okay?" I asked him.

He nodded.

"I wish you'd been a little more right."

He quietly said, "Everything will be okay, Bernie." After a moment he added, "Sometimes a seed has to fall to the earth and die, before it comes to life."

I kind of sucked in my breath and looked over my shoulder. But, like I said, the kids were long gone.

"You all right?" he asked.

"Yeah," I sort of croaked while sort of lying. "I'm fine."

"Good," he said. "Because I have one more thing left to do. Do you think you can help me with it?"

CHAPTER TWENTY

D

R

A

A

D

I

L

"Dr. Aadil. Dr. Aadil?"

At first I thought I was dreaming as a pair of hands shook me.

"Dr. Aadil, are you awake?"

I attempted to open my eyes, but the Reverend had recently increased my dosage of Propofol. No need for a jail cell when we have modern pharmaceuticals. And no, the irony of being imprisoned by the same drug I prescribe to help my patients was not lost on me.

"Dr. Aadil?"

A clumsy hand pried open my left eye. When my vision finally focused I saw Bernard Goldstein smiling down at me. "Dr. Aadil?"

"Ber . . ." My tongue was useless, swollen leather. "Berrrrr...nar?"

He grinned. "And Max," he whispered.

I squinted until I saw Maxwell Portenelli standing beside him.

"Hello, Doctor."

I groaned and closed my eye.

Bernard reopened it. "We've come to rescue you. If that's okay."

I rolled my head toward the door. It was ajar, but no light came from the hallway.

"Where . . ." I tried speaking again as Maxwell pulled off the blanket and slipped on my shoes. ". . . guard?"

"He's in the next bedroom with the Reverend's assistant," Bernard said. "They're having a nice time dancing to all that pretty music."

I strained to listen but heard nothing.

"Let's go," Maxwell whispered as he helped me sit up. He slipped his shoulder under mine and somehow between the three of us, I managed to stand. My consciousness had returned, but not much more. With effort we arrived at the door. Maxwell checked the hallway before we exited. When we reached the apartment's front door, they quietly opened it and we slipped out. Once we reached the stairway we started the arduous two flights down to the lobby.

"Why . . ." I whispered.

"Why what?" Bernard asked.

I motioned to what they were doing.

"Because you're our friend. And because God told

Max to do it, right Max?"

Maxwell gave no answer.

"Max?"

He shook his head and whispered, "No."

Bernard seemed surprised. "What? Then why–"

"Because it's the right thing to do."

Even in my state I could hear the resignation in his voice.

We continued down the steps.

Bernard, never a fan of silence, said, "But God is talking to you again, right?"

"No," Maxwell said.

"I . . . don't understand." Bernard sounded confused.

Maxwell gave no answer.

"Is He mad at you?"

Maxwell shook his head.

"Then why–"

"Sometimes . . ." Maxwell readjusted my weight and continued, "Sometimes to make our roots go deeper, God lets us go through dry times."

Bernard nodded. "Right." Then added, "What does that mean?"

Maxwell shook his head. "I'm not sure. But those were His exact words . . . before He stopped talking. "'The season of drought will make your faith grow deeper.'"

"Wow, that's cool," Bernard said, before adding, "I guess."

Maxwell nodded.

"So He's not mad at you?"

He gave no answer, which did nothing to impede the conversation.

"Max?"

"He doesn't get mad at us, Bernie. He got mad at Trashman, instead."

"Oh yeah," Bernard giggled. "I forgot."

We arrived at the bottom of the stairs and crossed through the tiny lobby with its single, flickering fluorescent. Before he opened the door, Maxwell turned to me and asked, "How are you? Better?"

I may have nodded, I don't remember. But I do remember him seeing the gash on my face and the look of compassion filling his eyes.

"Max," Bernard whispered, "shouldn't we be going?"

He continued staring.

"Max?"

He nodded. Then, ever so gently, he reached out and put his hand over my wound. It was still quite tender and I flinched at the touch. But his hand remained and I watched as he closed his eyes and began moving his lips. Bernard crowded in closer to watch. The moment lasted only a few seconds before Maxwell finished praying and withdrew his hand.

The look of disappointment on their faces said it all. Whatever they'd hoped for, had not happened.

With resolve, Maxwell turned to the lobby door and pushed it open. The night was cold and foggy. The empty street told me it was late.

"Where . . ." I coughed.

"Are we taking him to camp?" Bernard asked.

Maxwell shook his head.

"Where . . . going?" I said.

Before he could answer, a pair of headlights appeared through the fog.

"Max?" Bernard sounded nervous.

The lights approached.

"Max . . . we shouldn't be out in the open like this."

The beams flipped to high, so bright I had to look down.

"Max!"

There was the squelch of siren and the street filled with the flashing red and blue

lights of the police car.

"You'd better go, Bernie," Max said.

Bernard tugged at me harder, trying to move us faster.

"No," Max said, "just you."

"But–"

The car pulled to the curb, it's lights still blinding.

"Run, Bernie."

"Not without you."

"Yes, without me."

The front door opened.

"Run, Bernie. Run now!"

"But–"

Maxwell pulled me off Bernard's shoulder so he bore all of my weight. "Now!"

Confused, but always affable, Bernard started backing away, slowly at first.

"Run!"

Then faster.

"Go!"

Finally he turned and bolted, Maxwell shouting after him.

"Run, Bernie! Run!"

CHAPTER TWENTY-ONE

B
E
R
N
A
R
D

I felt real bad about leaving Max. So bad that I didn't get to sleep until real late. And by all the tossing and turning I heard around camp, I'm betting the rest of our friends felt that way, too. But when I finally did get to sleep it was a good thing, because that's when the two of us got back together again.

We were hiking up some mountain trail for about forever which, I'm not sure how long that is in dream time, but it was pretty long. There was also lots of snow, but it wasn't cold. And the closer we got to the top, the more I heard voices.

"Who's that?" I asked.

Max smiled that smile of his which made me smile back. It was nice to see it again.

"It sounds like a party," I said.

He nodded. "A celebration."

"For what?"

"For you."

"For me? What did I do?"

"It's not what you did, Bernie, it's who you are."

Just about then we reached the top. We rounded a thick grove of fir trees and there, not fifty feet away, were all sorts of people in all sorts of clothing. They looked a lot different from each other, but they all had one thing in common . . . they were singing and dancing and eating and drinking. Okay, that's more than one thing, but math was never my specialty, especially in dreams.

"There he is!" someone shouted.

Everyone turned and spotted us. I wasn't sure what to do so I sort of smiled and gave a little wave.

They grinned and gave a bigger wave.

I grinned bigger and waved harder.

They grinned harder and waved even bigger. It was kind of fun, except for the part of not knowing what was going on.

"Max?"

He chuckled. "Just keep walking."

When we reached the crowd they began to part. Everyone was still smiling and still waving which, I don't want to complain, but it was kind of wearing out my arm (and my lips). The shorter folks squeezed in front of the taller ones for a better look. Some of the moms and dads hoisted their children onto their shoulders. And it was all about us.

Pretty soon we started to hear wind. But it wasn't all soft and quiet like the breeze with the flute music. Instead, it roared like a freight train, like what they say tornados do. There was no other sound, unless you count the screaming and howling. Talk about creepy. Creepier still, you couldn't feel it blowing. Seriously. Not a leaf was stirring.

"Max?"

"Hang on, Bernie."

The screaming grew louder . . . and creepier.

"Shouldn't I be waking up about now?"

"We're almost there."

I had no idea where there was, and I was even less sure I wanted to be there. The last of the crowd parted and I finally saw it . . . a miniature tornado. Only it was more like a tunnel, straight up and down, and about thirty feet across.

"What is it?" I yelled.

He motioned for me to look at the wall of wind, which I did.

Actually, there were lots of walls, one inside the other. Some were spinning one direction, others were spinning the opposite. And trapped inside each wall were monsters, every sort you could imagine, and a few you don't want to. Like the crowd, they were all staring at me. Some were tiny, others big. Some spiny, others slimy. Some had grotesque faces on animal bodies, others had animal faces on grotesque bodies. But each and every one was being twisted and stretched by the wind. They scratched and clawed against it so they could stay up front and stare at me. But that only lasted a second before they were whisked away, only to circle and return another moment before they were dragged off again, and again. Around and around. I stepped closer for a better look. Along with all the monsters there were a few humans. People I knew. Like from the hospital.

Or even from my childhood.

I turned to Max and shouted, "What is this place?"

"Just listen," he yelled.

"All I hear is wind and screaming monsters."

"Listen inside! Listen to what's playing inside!"

I closed my eyes and strained to hear past all the commotion until, finally, there it was. The flute. It was faint, but unmistakable. I opened my eyes and squinted hard, trying to see through the walls of wind all the way to the center. Besides the monsters, everything else was a smeary blur, except . . . I squinted harder. For the briefest second I caught a glimpse of something in the middle. A person.

"Trashman!" I shouted. "What's Trashman doing in there?"

"Waiting for you."

"For me?"

One rude creature with more than the usual amount of warts and horns appeared directly in front of me. I jumped back. He hung on just long enough to snarl and show some fangs that needed serious orthodontistry before he was whisked away.

I turned to Max. "Trashman wants me to go into that?"

"No. He wants you to join him."

I didn't exactly see the difference. And I didn't exactly have time to ask because, suddenly, the tunnel bulged toward us. Before I could leap back, it sucked me into the first wall of wind. The outer one.

"MAX . . ."

But Max had managed to stay outside. Now I was in the wall of wind, spinning round and round, with the creepy critters on every side. The good news was they couldn't seem to touch me. Not that they didn't try. But each time one reached out a claw to shake my hand, or rip off my face, it was dragged away, while doing the usual screamings and screechings.

I shot past Max again and shouted for help. He didn't have time to answer. But when I came back around, he yelled, "Listen for the music! Follow it to Trashman!"

I looked into the center where I could just barely make out the little fellow. When I flew past again Max yelled, "You can do it! Just like the boulders in your other dream. Use the music!"

Of course I didn't have the faintest idea what he was talking about. But I knew

Trashman was somehow a part of it, so I began pushing and shoving at the inside edge of the first wall to try and get to him. Nothing worked. There was no way I could break through. And it didn't help to have all those monsters around.

"The music!" Max shouted as I shot past again. "Join the music!"

Of course he still made no sense, which I guess is okay for dreams. But it did get me to remember what I did with the boulders. So I listened real hard for the music. Once I heard it, I joined in. I started to hum a little and then louder, just like with the boulders. Then I tried pushing against the wall again, humming like my life depended on it (which it probably did) until, suddenly, I broke through and:

WOOSH . . . "Ow!" I was inside the next wall being yanked in the opposite direction.

It may have been a new wall and a new direction but my monster neighbors were pretty much the same. The only difference was the music. It was louder. Oh, and one other thing. I saw my mother.

"Mom!" I shouted.

I fought through the wind toward her. We hadn't seen each other since I was about seven, way back when she deserted me at the mental health facility. Not that I blamed her. It was real hard raising a kid by yourself, especially when he was a "nut job" which was her favorite pet name for me. Anyway, the closer I got, the better I could see her face. To my surprise, tears were streaming down it. Thanks to the marvels of dream logic, I knew she was crying because of what she'd done to me. So I pushed and swam past by one cranky creature after another, until I got close enough for her to hear me.

"It's okay!" I shouted. "I understand!"

She cocked her head to the side like she heard my voice, but couldn't see me.

"I'm right here, Mom!" I waved my arms in front of her. "Right here!" But no amount of waving helped. She just couldn't see me. "It's really okay!" I yelled. "Don't cry! I understand! Mom, please don't cry." My own eyes were beginning to burn with tears. "I forgive you!"

Her face brightened. Not much. But enough to make me think she'd heard. So I kept shouting. "It's true! It's me, Bernie. And I forgive you! I really forgive you! Honest!"

She blinked and started to smile when, suddenly, there was a bright flash of light and she was whisked away – but not by the wind. Instead, she was whisked *out* of the wind. One moment she was inside, the next moment, *FLASH,* she was outside, standing next to Max.

The *FLASH* was pretty bright and made all my traveling buddies inside the wind scream louder, like their pain had gotten worse. It also made the music louder. I turned back to the center, toward Trashman, and listened to it. I closed my eyes and began humming with it as I moved to the edge of the wall and pushed against it until—

WOOSH . . . "Ow!" I was inside the next wall, spinning the opposite direction. Talk about whiplash. The good news was the music had gotten even louder.

Like before, I swam and ducked past the monsters until I was surprised even more to spot Biff, (or was it Brock?) the attendant at Sisco Heights Mental Health Facility. He's the one who always did those mean things to me which I pretended never to notice though you'd have to be crazier than me not to. He was also crying, just like Mom. And just like Mom, I knew the reason.

"It's okay Biff, or is it Brock?" I shouted. "I forgive you, too!"

He looked up, startled.

I knew he couldn't see me so I kept yelling. "Really, it's okay! I really forgive you! Really!"

There was another *FLASH* and suddenly he was also outside the tunnel standing next to Mom and Max. The screamings grew even louder. So did the music. I swam to the edge of the next wall, humming all the harder and pushing until—

WOOSH – "Ow!" I was closer, and spinning the opposite direction.

That's when I spotted Jamal, my friend from the hospital who took lots of pleasure in rearranging my face whenever he could. Like Mom and Biff (or was it Brock), he looked real sad and real guilty. There were no tears (you have to know how to cry to get those), but he definitely looked unhappy. And I definitely knew why.

"It's okay," I shouted, "I forgive you!"

And, *FLASH,* he joined the others outside. And just like before, the screaming and the music grew even louder.

I swam to the edge of the next wall, humming, pushing, and–

WOOSH – "Ow!" (I hope Max knows a good chiropractor).

It could have gone on like this forever, and maybe it did, but I was definitely running out of night. I was also running out of walls. So I hummed and pushed and hummed and pushed until I tumbled out of the last wall and fell onto what seemed to be a glass floor. I mean it looked like glass. And it felt like glass. But when you stared down at it, it was like you were on the world's clearest and deepest ocean . . . that had no bottom.

I stayed there a moment on my hands and knees trying to catch my breath. Everything was completely still. No wind. No screaming. No music. Only my gasping for air. I noticed Trashman kneeling down beside me. When I looked up he was smiling just like he used to, way back when he was alive.

"Buenas noches, amigo?"

I nodded and looked back at the walls of wind filled with the shrieking creatures. They were still there, but you couldn't hear them. You couldn't hear anything.

"Wow," I finally said. "Not exactly your every day, run-of-the mill dream, is it?"

He just grinned.

"What were those things?" I asked. "Those

monsters? There was sure a lot of them."

He shook his head and answered in broken English. "Not really."

I frowned. "I don't want to be argumentative, but they were everywhere. Talk about being outnumbered."

"That is not true," he said. "With me, you will always be in the majority."

I nodded but had no idea what he was talking about which I guess was good because it meant things were finally getting back to normal. He stood up and reached down to me. I was grateful for the help and reached out to take his hand. That's when I noticed the hole in it.

CHAPTER TWENTY-TWO

S
A
F
F
R
O
N

"So I basically just fully agree with what the Reverend says."

I throw a look to Joey who motions me to keep starin' at his cell phone and keep talkin, so I do.

"I personally spent time with him and he's a great man a God who really knows his shi– stuff. Ain't nobody gets the Ancient Text like him. And if God says it's time to rise up and smite His enemies, then it's time we rise up and kick some serious butt."

I glance across the room to where the Reverend is sittin' and noddin'. Been a long time since I cared what any man thinks, but for some reason this is different.

The rest of the group is here, too, standin' behind Joey. With Max gone and the way things are heatin' up, all of us are glad to be a part of somethin' this important. The jails are pretty full now, mostly street people. How many of 'em are real believers and followers of the Reverend, who knows. But like he's been sayin' in all his podcasts, "Those who ain't against us is for us." And believe me there are plenty a "*fors*." More growin' every day.

Course the cops still have the upper hand with their water cannons and tear gas and all. But we got the numbers. And not just street people. More and more civilians, regular folks sayin,' enough is enough. It's just like the Reverend predicted, we're becomin' a revolution.

"Max." Winona whispered over to me, "Don't forget about Max."

I nod, rememberin' what we'd discussed.

"We all seen them videos," I said, still talkin' to the cell phone. "How the government's attackin' innocent people. And we all know how they arrested and are illegally holdin' Maxwell Portenelli, the inspirational force behind this great and glorious movement."

It was a stretch, but the Reverend says nothin's wrong with a little dressin' up the facts if it's for the common good. I keep goin'.

"He loved the Reverend. We sat together under his teachin' and he had some real fine discussions with him. So, for those of you who followed him at the beginnin', who first burned them lists, *now* is the time to step it up and join us."

Winona, who was watchin' the time, motioned for me to hurry – somethin' 'bout them tracking the call.

I glanced down at the last part which we wrote up so I wouldn't make a mistake:

"So let us rise up together. In memory of Maxwell Portenelli, let us rise up with the Reverend and join forces. Join with us as we throw off the yoke of our oppressors and stand up for God. We are the people He has called. We are the people who are righteous." I gave a little pause for what they call dramatic effect. "We are the people of God! And now, this very hour, let us stand up for His glory! Now is the time to live or die! Now is the time to live or die for the glory of God!"

I stare at the phone a second or two before Joey turns it off.

"Fantástico!" Ralphy clapped his hands from over in the corner. Others joined in and I shoot 'em a frown 'til the Reverend speaks up.

"You have done us a great service, Saffron. Hundreds of thousands, perhaps millions across this great land of ours, will soon hear your message."

I nod and look down.

But he keeps goin'. "It is one thing for the people to hear my voice. But to hear someone like yourself, the salt of the earth, express herself with such passion – that, my dear sister, will make all the difference in the world."

Bernie chimes in. "She was really good, wasn't she?"

I cut him an angry look.

"Yes," the Reverend says. And when I glance up I see him smilin' down at me. "An inspiration for us all."

I feel my face gettin' all hot like some school girl. I must a shook my head 'cause he goes on, "You don't believe me?" Before I can answer, he gets to his feet. "Come. Allow me to show you something." He heads out of the tiny apartment and the rest of us follow. It's the second place he's moved to since we visited with Max. And only a few of us more privileged types knows the location.

Pretty soon we come to a door down in the basement. He knocks twice, pauses, then three times. Someone opens it and not fifteen feet away, I see JJ. He's workin' a crowbar, openin' some wooden crate. He's all spruced up and clean, not even wearin' his beard.

"JJ?" I says.

He looks up and grins. "Hey, babe."

"What you doin' here?"

"Jes helpin' the cause." The crate creaks open. He pulls off the lid and there in shredded newspaper is a bunch of rifles. Not the huntin' type, but the army type. Just like the two dozen or so against the wall.

"Where'd you get them?" I ask.

"I gots connections." He flashes his semi-toothless grin and gets back to the crate.

The Reverend says, "Jonathan has become a real asset to us."

I was hard pressed for words. I guess we all were. 'Cept Bernie.

"Are you a believer now?" he says.

JJ looks up to him and grins. "Ain't it a miracle? I seen the light. Thanks to Saffron, I have seen the light and I have changed my ways." He turns to me. I give him a hard look, but he just keeps grinnin'.

"How many do we have there, Jonathan?" the Reverend asks.

"This here's twelve. Plus them over there, makes

thirty-seven. But there's plenty more where these come from. If we got the cash."

"God will provide."

"Cool," JJ says.

"Well, keep up the good work, my friend."

"You bet," JJ says. "Praise the Lord."

The Reverend turns and we all start to leave but JJ, he ain't quite done yet.

"Hey, babe?"

I slow and turn to him.

"Later. When I'm all done, what say me and you get together?" He tries to grin, but it comes out a leer. "You know, a little romantic reunion?"

I feel my face gettin' hot again, but the Reverend, he steps in. "Jonathan, I am afraid you have misjudged Saffron. She is no longer that sort of woman."

I catch my breath. Can't help myself.

"She belongs to God now. The lady you see before you today is clean, and pure and righteous."

JJ stutters. "Right, no, of course. I get it. I was just sayin'—"

"I know exactly what you were saying, Jonathan. And until you cleanse your wicked heart, I must ask that you refrain from making contact with this woman of God. Have I made myself clear?"

"Oh, right, sure. No offense, I gets it."

"Good." The Reverend looked down at me and smiled.

I look up and can't help smilin' back.

As we turn to join the others I can feel JJ's eyes burnin' a hole in my back but I don't care. The Reverend holds the door open for me like a real gentleman and gently puts his hand in the small of my back to guide me through.

CHAPTER TWENTY-THREE

D
R

A
A
D
I
L

"You lied to me! I trusted you and you lied to me!"

Alexis Portenelli was on me the moment the doors to Mercy General hissed open and I stepped into the cold drizzle. Besides changing the dressing on the gash on my face, they'd been running a battery of tests making sure that, other than a bad case of head lice, I hadn't picked up any other souvenirs from my vacation to the Tenderloin.

The girl looked as terrible as I felt. Face drawn, no makeup, hair disheveled, unwashed. "That wasn't the deal!" she raged.

Which deal? I thought. The one I'd made with the mayor's office? The one where they played me? The one that exchanged Maxwell's freedom for my own? Pick a deal, any deal.

"Ms. Portenelli," I sighed as we started down the steps, "the situation is in continual flux. No one can predict how things change from day to day."

"I want to see him."

"I'm not even allowed to see him."

"He's my father."

"Current circumstances make that impossible."

"He's not a circumstance." She grabbed my arm and pulled me to a stop. "He's my father."

I took a patient breath. "Ms. Portenelli, in case you haven't noticed, your father has single-handedly brought this city to the brink of disaster."

She blinked.

"Look around you. San Francisco is on the verge of a civil war and it was your father who started it."

"All he did was talk about . . . God's love."

"Yes, well–" I pulled away from her and continued down the steps. "Apparently no one got the memo."

She shouted after me. "I'll sue! His constitutional rights are being totally ignored."

Ooo, I thought, *someone's read a book.*

"I'll sue the city. I'll sue the Department of Religious Affairs. I'll sue you. Malpractice. Incompetence. Intent to do harm!"

Not bothering to slow, I called over my shoulder, "You have no case."

"It doesn't matter. Our lawyers will keep you in court the rest of your pathetic little life!" She yelled and heads turned but I kept walking. "You're a fraud,

Doctor! A puppet of the State. And I'll spend every dime of our company to make sure the world knows it!"

That was it. I'd been through enough. I didn't need to be lectured by an entitled, self-absorbed brat. I spun around and headed back up the steps. "What exactly are you trying to prove?"

She was startled, unsure how to answer. I pressed in.

"What's your game?"

"He's . . . my father."

"Your father is a man you barely knew. Who barely knew you. He loved his business more than he ever loved his family. He treated his employees better than he treated you."

"He . . . loved me."

"Now who's lying? He never gave you the time of day. And what was he to you but a credit card that never maxed out?"...Okay, I may have stepped over the line. So sue me. No wait, take a number.

I paused for a response. She swallowed hard and looked away.

"What?"

"He's . . . different." Her voice began to clog. "He's not the same."

I set my jaw, refusing to be drawn in.

"You saw him those last days in the hospital . . . when he said goodbye to me." She took an uneven breath. "You've seen him on the internet. What he's been saying, what he believes."

"And you honestly think—"

"I don't know what I think!" She took an angry swipe at her eyes. "But that man, he's . . . my father."

CHAPTER TWENTY-FOUR

B
E
R
N
A
R
D

"So which will it be?" Winona said. "Max or the Reverend."

I looked at her and then I looked to the rest of the group who looked at me. We were all huddled under our overpass wearing blankets and drinking cold, watery oatmeal that Chloe had cooked from what the nice folks at O.R.B. gave us. We could have got something from the soup kitchens but they were making everybody register and get their pictures taken which made Joey and some of the others nervous. We could have built a fire, but the way they were cracking down and destroying all the camps made Saffron nervous. And me? I wasn't nervous, but I really missed Max. I know everyone was trying to help me feel better, but the way they kept saying all the things Max had been wrong about, well, to be honest, it really didn't make things easier.

"You believe everything the Reverend says, do you not?" Ralphy asked. He ran his hand over his eyes. He did that a lot now that he didn't have goggles to adjust.

"You bet," I said.

"Then how can you believe Señor Max?"

"Because . . . he's my friend."

Saffron gave a heavy sigh from her rocker. It looked like she wanted to swear but we all knew she couldn't.

"Look, Bernie," Joey said. "You heard what the Reverend said to him, right?"

"Right."

"And you agree with the Reverend, right?"

"Right."

"So it's wrong to say Max is right when you know he's wrong, right?"

I started to answer, then frowned. "Could you repeat the question?"

Winona, who'd been scanning the internet on Joey's cell phone said, "Doesn't matter. He's been arrested, so that's that."

There was a low rumble down on the freeway. Chloe leaned over to me and whispered, "Four."

I recognized the sound from before and nodded. It was the third National Guard truck coming into the city.

Ralphy turned to Winona. "What do you mean by, 'that is that?'"

144

She answered, "The man was wrong and God is punishing him. End of story."

I shifted on my crate. "I don't want to be rude, but. . ."

She looked at me.

"Didn't Max say God got mad at Trashman so He wouldn't get mad at us?"

Everyone kind of paused until Darcy spoke up. "You're ducking the question, moron."

"You're right," I said. "Sorry. What was it again?"

"Who's side are you on?" Joey said.

"Side?"

"I count three," Joey said. "The Reverend . . . Max . . . or the government. Which side are you on?"

I shrugged. "They've all got their nice qualities – though the government is a little harder to like with all their clubs and Tasers and stuff."

"Hang on," Winona said. "Listen up." She motioned for us to gather around the cell phone which we did. It was another news report.

"Hey, that's Carrie Phillips," I cried. Then I glanced over to Chloe to make sure she wasn't jealous.

"Shhh," Saffron said.

"Sorry," I said, "I just–"

"Shhh," the others said.

I nodded and moved in closer to listen.

"–viewer discretion advised as we look at these candid, cell phone videos shot during Maxwell Portenelli's nights on the street. Videos that have been obtained exclusively by KBBS."

We stared at the tiny screen and saw a jerky video that was kind of grainy of Max lying on a bare mattress. But the mattress wasn't the only thing bare. He was pretty naked, too, except for the blurry parts that covered his nakedness where he wasn't wearing any clothes. On top of him was a pretty girl like you see on the billboards only she wasn't doing such pretty things. I'd seen photos of that stuff in the magazines my old roommate kept under his mattress and, between you and me, well, they were kind of confusing and definitely not pretty.

Another video came on. Max was still blurry in his naked parts, only now there were two different ladies with even more blurriness. They were laughing and giggling like what they were doing was supposed to be fun.

"No wonder God wasn't talking to him," Joey said.

"Shhh," everyone said.

They showed another video. It was getting harder to watch. In fact, my stomach was starting to get a little queasy which, at least this time, I was pretty sure had nothing to do with Chloe's cooking.

They cut to another video. The picture was all shadowy, but it looked like Max sitting at a metal table talking to a couple nice looking men. Carrie explained what was happening:

"*And, now as Mr. Portenelli returns to the care and treatment of his doctors, he has agreed to assist the police in helping to find leaders of O.R.B., an organization he insists he never supported.*"

The picture switched to a bumpy video of policemen running up some apartment stairs that looked exactly like–

"That's the Reverend's," Joey said.

But instead of "Shhhing" him, we all watched as the men broke down the door and the camera followed them into the Reverend's first apartment –

the one where we all met to help Max. But of course, it was empty because he had moved a couple times since then. But it didn't stop some of us from getting upset.

"He ratted him out," Darcy shouted.

"Or at least tried to," Joey agreed.

But of everyone there, Saffron was the most upset. She kind of leaped to her feet and started to pace. But only for a moment. Pretty soon, she turned and started down the steep ramp toward the city.

"Saffron?" Joey called. "Where are you going?"

She didn't say a word but just kept on walking.

Carrie was back on the screen. *"Neither the Reverend nor his cache of arms were present at the location. However, according to our sources, authorities are tightening the manhunt and closing in. Meanwhile, according to the Mayor's office, Mr. Portenelli has, and I quote, 'Been helpful and forthcoming in identifying the various locations of the homeless camps where the Reverend's supporters dwell.'"*

As she talked, they cut to another video. It showed the police burning and destroying another camp just like they'd been doing plenty of. But we didn't watch long because suddenly Chloe cried out, "One! Two! Three!"

I turned. She wasn't counting National Guard trucks. She was looking down the ramp and counting police cars sliding to a stop below us. We watched, unsure what we were supposed to do, as doors flew open and officers hopped out. It wasn't until they started toward us, that Winona had a plan.

"Run!" she yelled.

It made a lot of sense, so we took off. Well, most of us. Nelson had to first gather his library books. And I took a moment to pick up our dirty cups and dishes so we wouldn't leave a mess.

Then there was Darcy. She just stood there shouting at us. "Go! Go!"

"What about you?" I said.

"I'll be there. Just go!"

The last thing I wanted to do was make Darcy mad (it'd never turned out well in the past) so I ran. Not far behind me I heard the officers arriving, knocking over our crates, tearing down our tarps and doing your basic destruction kind of things.

When I caught up to the rest of the group, Chloe, who was kind of panicking, shouted, "Where do we go?"

"Let's find Max," I yelled. "He can tell us what we're to—"

"He's in jail," Joey shouted.

"He's the one responsible," Ralphy yelled.

"No!" I said. "He'd never hurt us."

"See for yourself!" Joey shouted.

I looked over my shoulder and then slowed to a stop. We were about thirty yards away, except for Darcy. She'd stayed behind and was shouting and yelling at one of the officers who was sloshing something from a big red container all over our stuff.

"No." I shook my head. "Max would never allow this!"

"How do you think they found us?" Joey yelled. "This is Max's doing. He told them! He is responsible!"

I watched as another officer lit a long, metal lighter.

Darcy raced toward him, shouting and screaming. But he didn't seem to care. He just bent down, touched the lighter to the ground and, *WOOSH,* it started a fire. It really spread fast, crawling over everything . . . our crates, Saffron's rocker, everything. By the time Darcy got to him, it was too late. But that didn't stop her from swearing and swinging at him.

"Darcy!" Winona shouted.

She was too busy to hear . . . until another officer figured she'd shared enough of her deeply-rooted feelings. He came at her from behind with a baton and, without even bothering to introduce himself, he hit her hard on the shoulder. She crumbled to her knees but didn't fall over.

"Darcy!" I yelled.

The officers looked toward us.

Let's go," Joey shouted. He grabbed Chloe's and my arms and pulled us forward. "Come on, let's get out here!"

But I didn't move. I could only watch in concern as the officer raised his club again. But I wasn't concerned for Darcy. It was for the poor officer who didn't know what he was getting into. She sprang at him from below like a football lineman. He stumbled backwards and fell. That's when she leaped on top of him and tried to get the club out of his hands. When he didn't let go, she settled for grabbing something from his belt. But he was a lot stronger than you'd think and somehow managed to shove her off and then stagger to his feet.

Darcy got to her knees and saw him coming again, raising his club. That's when I saw the canister she was holding. The one she pointed at him. The one she'd grabbed from his belt. She pressed a button and it sprayed into his face, causing him to scream, claw at the air, and stumble backwards all over again. Some people never learn.

Darcy scampered to her feet and kept going at him, the steady stream of liquid never ending.

By now fire was all around them, but it didn't matter. Not to Darcy. Unfortunately, she didn't see the other officer. The one coming at her who had been lighting the fire.

"Look out!" I yelled, "Look out!"

She spun around and pointed the can at him so he could have a dose, too. She hadn't noticed the gun in his hand. And she didn't have time to stop or duck or run before he fired one, two, three times into her chest.

"Darcy!" I started toward her but Nelson and Joey both grabbed me.

She turned toward me. Through the wavering fire and heat I saw the look of shock on her face. And surprise. But she still wouldn't go down. Not until the officer stepped closer, placed the barrel of his pistol against the side of her head and fired.

"DARCY!"

She dropped to the ground.

"Let's go!" Joey shouted. "There's nothing we can do!"

I don't know what happened next. There wasn't any sound. I didn't hear anything. Not even Joey who was yelling right into my face. I couldn't hear him but I knew what he wanted. Someone was turning me around, pushing me forward. And, somehow, some way, I managed to run. I had no feeling in my legs or anywhere, but I was running. And starting to cry. Running and crying.

For how long, I don't know.

CHAPTER TWENTY-FIVE

A
L
E
X
I
S

"Wrong! So incredibly wrong. What rotting armadillo did you skin for this leather?"

"You said, you wanted—"

"And heels, really? Did anybody so much as look at my notes?"

"We thought—"

"You're not paid to think!"

"Lex."

I turned on Robert. "We've got ten days before N.Y. and this is what they're giving me?"

"Alexis."

"Did you see the handbags? Not even close!" I was on a downhill rant and couldn't find the brakes.

"Why do I kill myself when no one bothers to pay attention! Or maybe they're working for our competition." I spun to the minion. "Is that it Johnny, you and the kiddies trying to sabotage me?"

"I would never . . ." He grew whiny. "Why would you think that?"

"Why do you make me crap?"

"We just weren't sure what . . ." He took an uneven breath.

"What?"

He shook his head.

"Answer me! You just weren't sure what?"

He broke into a blubber. "We're doing the best we can."

"Ahh, is Jimmy gonna cry?"

"Alexis!" Robert turned to the hatchling. "You'll excuse us, Jeremy."

He sniffed and nodded. I finished my cig and lit another as he scooped up the shoes and limped out of the room. "Do you believe that?" I crossed to my desk and collapsed into my chair. "Have they the slightest clue of my vision?"

"Maybe if your vision didn't change every forty-eight hours."

"I want it perfect. Is that too much to ask?" I pulled a vile from my purse and tapped out a line.

"When's the last time you slept?"

"Yeah, right."

"And Troy Hudson?"

"No booty calls, til we get this thing put to bed. He understands." I sniffed up the candy and it burned like hell.

"You might want to cut down a little."

"It gives me focus." I wiped my nose and glanced

to the computer.

It had been nearly an hour since I checked the latest post. Definite progress. Drugs and booze are no problem for me. I'm not the addictive type. But when it came to info on Father, I couldn't get enough. It didn't help that they'd dedicated an entire YouTube channel to him with videos constantly popping up. True, most were rehash reposts, but every once in a while there was something new. And those were gold. Particularly the ones where he's talking with everyday people. I'd seen all the others – the "leaked" cop interviews, the infamous bedroom rompings (which the diehard devotees insisted were staged by a double). But the ones of him talking and listening to the people, those were the ones that got to me.

Media's nothing new to our family. Publicity, good or bad, is our bread and butter. But watching this man, the one I knew but didn't know, hearing him speak from his heart, seeing the compassion in his eyes . . . what daughter wouldn't want a dad like that? No agendas, no distractions. Just someone who acted like whoever he talked to was the most important person on earth. And with every kind word he spoke, every thoughtful smile he gave, I wanted more.

But we had a show in one and a half weeks. The company's future depended on me. There was no way I'd let Uncle Al and his spineless board of cowards sell us off to St. Cheron. We deserved better than that. Father deserved better. Even though it killed me, I forced myself to return back to task. Like father, like daughter? I guess it would depend on which father we're talking about.

There was a knock at the door and Robert called, "Enter."

A far-too-perky assistant poked her head in. "She's here."

Robert nodded and turned to me. "Show time."

"Right." I took a last drag from my ciggie, butted it out and rose. Show time was right. We passed the aquarium with its multiple cell phones and dying fish and headed out into the shop.

Robert called past the workers and cutting tables. "Vittoria, my dear. How good to see you."

Vittoria My Dear may or may not have responded. Who could tell behind the Imax-size shades? I kept quiet, letting Robert be the welcoming committee. "You look great," he said, arriving and giving her the obligatory kiss on the cheeks. Being adverse to frostbite, I didn't bother.

"How are you feeling?" he asked.

Without a word she reached into her Versace and pulled out a computer tablet.

Initially, her legal said she'd get rid of the kid if we stood inside the clinic's room and were forced to watch the procedure. Twisted and weird? Welcome to my world. We countered with simply asking the clinic to supply us with a receipt, to which her team countered with. . . well, cutting to the chase and after paying a few months salary in legal bills, we finally agreed we would look at her before and after sonograms. Thanks for visiting my reality and please stop by the gift shop for more twisted and weird on your way out.

Vittoria set the tablet on the nearest cutting table and, except for the TV which droned quietly on the far wall, the entire shop fell silent. Although none of the underlings stopped working, every eye and ear was focused on this year's winner of the Cannes Best

Actress Award. She did not disappoint. Summoning all of her training, she reached down and with great courage, snapped on the computer. A color-enhanced video filled the screen.

I don't care how many times you've seen an unborn child, there's something magical about them. And yeah, it looked more alien than human, but there were still those arms, legs, that head and glimpses of a face.

Vittoria's voice dropped to a hoarse whisper. "That's my baby . . . my child."

I kept staring at the screen, unable to pull my eyes from it. But it wasn't over. She reached down to the tablet and hit a couple keys.

"And this . . ." it was the same video but without the baby. "This is what I have now."

Even though I was being played, the impact caught me off guard. Maybe it was the coke, the sleepless nights, the whatever, but I couldn't look away. All I could do was stare at the emptiness, the lonely, vacant emptiness.

Then something happened that even Vittoria could not have orchestrated. Even though it was faint and no one else seemed to notice, I heard Dr. Aadil's voice. I glanced up and saw he was on the TV screen across the room. He sat in a news studio being interviewed.

Vittoria's voice began to tremble. "This is all I have left."

I turned back to the empty sonogram as she continued.

"Nothing. Do you understand what I'm saying?"

I heard Father's voice and looked up to see the familiar footage of him talking to street people.

"Nothing." Vittoria tapped the computer. "I am as empty here . . ." She raised her hand and tapped her chest, "as I am here. Do you understand? *Do you understand me?*" Tears streamed from under her glasses. "I am empty!"

I looked back at the sonogram. I stared at the image and heard my father's voice. I couldn't make out his words but I heard their compassion.

Vittoria cried, "Empty!"

The room shifted. I reached for the table.

"I have nothing. My child is dead!"

I stared at the emptiness on the computer. I heard my father.

"I murdered my baby!" She began sobbing. "I murdered my baby and I have nothing!"

Thankfully, Dr. Aadil's voice came back on the TV. But it was too late. When I looked up, my vision was already growing white. My face broke into a sweat and I gripped the table tighter.

"Nothing!"

No. I would not give her the satisfaction. I was a Portenelli. My father's daughter. I clung to the table.

"He is dead. I murdered my baby and I have . . ."

Her voice began to fade. So did the room. But I hung on. I was a Portenelli and I hung on . . . until my legs buckled and betrayed me.

CHAPTER TWENTY-SIX

D
R

A
A
D
I
L

I rested my head against the cold, glass window and stared out of my apartment. Not far away, a half dozen vandals were busy turning over a car. Further up the street, a storefront was burning. Those naive, innocent shopping cart fires had grown into something far more serious. O.R.B. had successfully turned Maxwell Portenelli into the inspiration and poster child of their revolution. And no amount of disinformation the city pumped into the media, seemed to help. Not even the trusted words of his faithful and loyal doctor.

Of course I refused to watch any of my interviews. It was hard enough choking out the words the first time . . .

"Yes, he is improving and growing healthier every day. . ."

"Yes, he has recanted his previous statements, owing them to his illness . . ."

"Yes, he is strongly opposed to the Reverend's position and pleads that the Reverend and his followers disband . . ."

What a load of bovine feces. To know what was going on inside Maxwell Portenelli's head, you'd have to visit Maxwell Portenelli. But that was one prize the State was going to protect at any cost – especially from doctors who might be struck with inconvenient bouts of integrity.

"Trust me," the Mayor had said earlier. "When this all blows over, your efforts will not be forgotten."

Which was precisely what I was afraid of.

I rolled my forehead against the cool glass. What I wouldn't give for another drink. But I'd run out hours ago and this was definitely not the time to be wandering the streets.

And what did he mean, "blow over?" Had he paid no attention to the Religious Wars of the past? Did no one in his office understand from history that persecution was the quickest way to fan the zealot's flame? If we'd learned just one thing during all those years of violence, it was the Department's slogan: "Absorb, Not Oppose." You control extremists with the carrot. You subtly purchase cooperation, suggesting incremental compromises that sound modern and progressive.

And, yes, you use the media, but not with the Mayor's heavy, ham-fisted approach. You begin with entertainment – innocent programs encouraging the opposition to smile, even laugh at some of their idiosyncrasies. Once your foot's in the door, you gradually turn up the heat until even they begin to see the dangers of their beliefs.

That's how you scrub a culture of religion. You don't fight against it, you indulge and entertain people out of it.

But the Mayor, bless his politically ambitious heart, had chosen to forgo the carrot and resort to a very large and brutal stick. It certainly provided all the sound bites he would need to run for Governor. Unfortunately, it could very well destroy his city, perhaps the entire state, in the process.

I pulled from the window and, out of habit, touched the bandage on my face. Strangely enough, there was no tenderness. I pressed more firmly, moving my fingers to the center. Still nothing. I frowned and took the twelve and a half steps from the kitchen to the bathroom and checked the mirror to take a look. Gently, I slipped my fingers under the tape and peeled it back. The only discomfort was the sticky adhesive.

Once the bandage was removed, I could only stare. There was no wound. I reached up, felt where it should be. Nothing. I leaned closer to the mirror for a better look. I touched and stretched the skin with my fingers. There was no sign of a cut. Not even a scar.

CHAPTER TWENTY-SEVEN

B
E
R
N
A
R
D

"Come on, Bernie, stay with the crowd," Joey shouted. "You're holding us back."

"But those policemen." I pointed up ahead to a line of officers standing all straight and neat. They wore real cool helmets and some great looking riot gear. "I really don't think they want us here."

"What are they going to do," Winona yelled back to me, "shoot us all?"

She had a pretty good point since there must have been two or three hundred of us and they'd probably run out of bullets first.

"Bernie!" Ralphy turned and shouted. "We must proceed. It is our sacred duty to stand up against the evils of unrighteousness."

I nodded and tried to move forward. Really, with all my might I tried, but I couldn't get my feet to cooperate.

There was the crash of another store window off to our right. And cheering. Lots of cheering.

"What about Max?" I yelled.

"What about him?" Winona shouted.

"I don't think he'd like us doing this. I don't think he–"

"Max killed Darcy!" Joey yelled. "He was the one responsible!"

I shook my head. "No, it was a policeman. I saw him. He was there in camp and he had a gun and–"

"Open your eyes, Bernie! I like Max. We all did. He was a good man, but–"

"'Was' is the operational word," Winona shouted. "He turned on us, Bernie. He turned on God. Now he's our enemy . . . and God's."

"'The friend of my enemy is my enemy,'"[47] Nelson quoted.

"But Max loves God."

"Maxwell Portenelli betrayed God!" Joey shouted.

There was more crashing and tinkering of glass and even more cheering. And smoke. Lots of smoke. And over on the next street it sounded like the fourth of July with what must have been tons of firecrackers going off.

The people around us surged forward and since we were jammed in pretty tight we surged, too. Well, the others surged. My feet still weren't cooperating. My head understood and was giving the orders, but my feet just kept thinking about Max.

"Bernie?" Even though she was holding my hand, I could barely hear Chloe over the noise. "Please?"

she shouted. "Please?" The urgency in her voice really got to me. And the pain in her eyes made my chest ache something awful. She kept tugging at my hand, trying to pull me forward. And I tried. Honest. But there was still that problem with my feet.

"Chloe . . ."

She looked up to me and I worked real hard to put my feelings into words. But I didn't have to. The look on her face and the tears in her eyes said she already knew. Probably better than me. But I had to try.

"He's . . . my friend."

She nodded and gave a sad sort of smile. She tried blinking back her tears, but they weren't any more cooperative than my feet. Still, even though we were getting pushed and jostled by the crowd, we managed to hang on to each other's hands . . . until some people pushed between us.

"Chloe!"

It did no good. Suddenly the whole crowd lunged forward and her hand slipped from mine.

"Chloe!"

When she came back into view, she was almost ten feet from me, being swept away.

"Chloe!"

She must have heard me. She had to have heard me. But she never turned to look back.

CHAPTER TWENTY-EIGHT

S
A
F
F
R
O
N

I wake up sitting on the bathroom floor, my back against the cold, tile wall. For a second I'm lost, 'til I get my bearings . . . 'til the guilt comes crashin' in – so heavy I can barely breathe.

"Harlot . . ." That was the word he'd mumbled.

I don't get up. No way I'm goin' back to bed. My body ain't sick. I got no flu or DT's. Nothin' physical. Just emotions. My insides so torn up I wanna heave some more, but can't.

"Jezebel . . ."

The words cut deep, but he'd been right. A leopard can't change his spots and neither can I. Makes no difference how hard I try, the badness just goes deeper and hides – crouchin', waitin' at the right time to explode back to the surface. A follower of God? Who am I foolin'?

Everything started innocent enough. Me worryin' 'bout the Reverend and runnin' over here to check on him. When they let me in, he's all kind and gracious, risin' up from the Ancient Text he'd been studyin' and standin' to greet me like a real gentlemen. Truth is, I ain't ever been treated that way. And how do I show my 'preciation? I start comin' on to him. I tell myself it's jus bein' friendly, but even then, I know better.

At first he's too good to know what's happin'. When he does, it's too late. He tries to resist, but good luck with that, him bein' a man and all. Part a me is outside, watchin', knowin full well what I'm doin'. But I don't stop. I play him like a fiddle 'til, just like clockwork, he's lockin' the door and we over on the bed doin' the nasty.

Even then my throat is all tight and I'm silently cussin' myself. But I still don't stop.

And when we done? He turns away. His body shudderin', voice whimperin' like some lost, little boy.

"You okay?" I say.

He makes sure I don't see his tears, but I know they're there. Then, gatherin' himself, he mumbles, "Harlot . . . Whore of Babylon . . ."

It hurts deep but I know he's right. I can dress up all I want, clean my language, play at bein' all holy. But it don't stick. No matter how hard I try, the real me is still there. And there ain't no God or religion can fix that. No lofty rules, no quotes from some book. I am what I am.

So I just laid there beside him, 'til the heavy breathin' tells me he'd drifted off into some fitful sleep. Not me. I just keep starin' up at the ceiling, thinkin' what I did, what I made him do. 'Til I gotta come in here to the john and hurl.

How long I'm sittin' here against the tile, I ain't sure. But eventually I pull myself together and rise to my feet. I see myself in the mirror, check my hair.

Harlot . . .

I finally step out into the room. He's snorin' away, sprawled out on the bed like some beached whale. The catch of the day. My catch.

Whore . . .

I gather my shoes and go out to the little kitchen, cold linoleum on my bare feet. The Ancient Text is still sittin' on the table right where we left it. Judge and jury. I slow to a stop, my throat gettin' tight again, my eyes burnin'. I swear and give 'em a swipe. My stomach's still twistin' but I don't move. I'm paralyzed, jus standin' there. Just me and the Ancient Text.

CHAPTER TWENTY-NINE

B
E
R
N
A
R
D

There was nothing left of the camp. Well, there was, but the nothing parts were scattered all around and pretty burned up. Our crates, the pieces of carpet, Saffron's rocker, everything was broken or burned or both. Even the garland on her Christmas bush had melted into the few skeleton branches that were left. The whole place smelled like smoke and wet charcoal. But I suppose, if you wanted to get technical, the whole city smelled that way.

I walked through the remains, kicking at burned pieces of whatever until my foot hit a book. I stooped down, brushed off the ashes and saw what was left of one of the phone books Nelson had been reading from the library. The outside parts were pretty much gone and I felt bad because he'd have to pay a pretty big fine. Good ol' Nelson. I really missed him. To be honest, I really missed everybody. Especially Chloe. It was like there was this giant hole in my chest and no amount of breathing, no matter how deep, could fill it.

Then, of course, there was Darcy. I wouldn't even go near the place where she'd been killed. It was hard to believe I'd never hear her sarcasm, or flinch whenever she made a fist again. But I probably wouldn't ever see anybody. We'd only been apart a day, but after all our months and years together, it felt like forever. Part of me wanted to go find them, but part of me knew it wouldn't work, not with them wanting to fight for the Reverend and all, and not with what they were trying to get me to believe about Max.

Max . . .

I took another deep breath. I tried my best not to think about him. And for the most part, I did pretty good . . . when I was awake. But not when I was asleep. Not when I dreamed. Because no matter what I did or where I slept, he and Trashman just keep showing up.

Last night was the perfect example. Once I'd found a place to sleep, in the back of the all night movie theater, and once I'd finished the bag of stale popcorn for dinner someone had left, I closed my eyes and drifted off.

Things picked up pretty much where they'd left off. I was back inside the middle chamber with all those walls of wind on the outside and Trashman helping me to my feet. As soon as I stood up, he threw his arms around me like we were old friends, which, I guess, in a way we were – though I was still kind of nervous about that whole kissing thing from the dream back at the hospital.

Anyway, when he held me, things really got interesting. Because that's when I started melting. Or maybe he was melting. It's hard to explain, but one way or another we were both getting really gooey and liquidy, until we began mixing into each other. But it didn't feel weird or bad or anything. In fact, it felt kind of good. Because the more we melted into each other, the more we started thinking and being like each other.

Don't get me wrong, I was still me. I mean, it's not like I wanted to start playing the flute or working for minimum wage or anything. Instead, the more we held each other, the more we were like each other and the more we thought like each other. And it was that thinking part that was the neatest because all Trashman seemed to think about was love . . . not sex love, but real love, like for people, for animals, for places – even love for those creepy monster things in the walls of wind. Seriously, I've never felt anything like it. It got to the point where I wanted to hug everything I saw, and everything I didn't. It was like my whole body was filled with his love. Except, and this was the tricky part, I no longer had a whole body.

It had disappeared into his.

And his had disappeared into mine.

We were still there, but we had melted into this blob of jelly-like liquid. You know, like those butterflies you see when they're in their cocoons changing from caterpillars. At first you figure they're just dead because the cocoon is dead, but when you cut it open (not you, but some neighborhood bully) you see there's nothing inside but liquid jelly. No caterpillar, no butterfly. And definitely no arms, legs or any of that. We were just this liquid blob floating above the glass floor. I wanted to ask Trashman about it, but that would mean having to find him, much less my mouth – not so easy when everything's all mixed together.

And then, just when there was so much love I couldn't take it, we exploded into blazing light. Brighter than the sun. Brighter than a hundred suns . . . and it was all coming from us!

I don't know how long it took to fade, and believe me it felt so good there was no hurry, but when it finally did, I noticed we were surrounded by thousands, maybe millions of other lights. But they weren't just lights, they were *living* lights. They were all different shapes and sizes, but you could tell they were alive by the way they danced . . . and sang. And here's the cool thing, actually everything was cool, but they sang the exact same music Trashman played on his flute. Only now the music was so clear and beautiful it gave you goose bumps, if you had a body to have goose bumps which, suddenly, I did. So did Trashman. Not only did we have bodies, but somehow I had changed clothes. I was wearing a long robe of purple and burgundy that shimmered and flashed like lightning. And Trashman? He was wearing the same brilliant, white light that all those singers wore, only about a billion times brighter.

I know this all sounds like I'd taken the wrong medication or something, but I'm only telling you what I saw . . . and heard . . . and felt. And, even though I knew it was only a dream, I kept thinking to myself, *Wow, this is sooo cool!*

To which Trashman answered, *Si, Si. Cool. Very cool!*

I turned to him. He looked as excited as a kid on Christmas morning.

You can hear me? I thought.

And you can hear me.

You're thinking English.

So are you.

He had a point. *Why are you so happy?* I thought. *Why is everybody so happy and excited?*

Because you have finally arrived.

I had no idea what he meant which meant things were getting back to normal. But not quite . . .

Trashman reached out for me to take his hand again. I took it but was kind of careful because of the hole and everything. He smiled and then turned me around to face a giant, glowing platform. At the top of it was an honest-to-goodness throne. It was super bright like everything else, but with different colors shooting from it, changing all the time – like a rainbow but a zillion times brighter and more colorful. In fact, some of the colors I'd never even seen before.

Ven, mijo. Trashman motioned me to the stairs that led up to it. I nodded and we started. There were only twelve, but with every step we took, the singing got deeper. Not deeper, like lower, but deeper like vibrating further and further inside me.

We were practically at the top when I stopped and turned to ask. *What about Max? He's still outside those walls.*

Trashman grinned. *He'll be here soon enough.* He motioned for us to continue.

Once we reached the top I sort of gasped, which is

exactly the thing you do when you notice that those singing lights you'd seen earlier, stretch on forever and ever . . . and that they're all looking at you.

I swallowed hard. *This is* . . . I tried to find the words but couldn't.

He laughed. *Si, Si.* And then, in English, he added, *And now you will sit.*

Sit? I said. *Where?*

He motioned to the blazing throne of colors. *With me.*

I swallowed. *This? This is your throne?*

Of course.

I glanced around then lowered my voice or thoughts or whatever, so I wouldn't hurt his feelings. *I thought you were a janitor.*

I am.

And a king?

Of course. He motioned back to the throne.

And you want me to sit here? I thought. *With you?*

Si.

I . . . I can't sit there.

Si. Si. Now you are ready. Now you will rule.

But . . .

If you do not sit with me, you cannot rule.

I was more confused than ever. *Rule over what?*

Everything. He grinned which kicked up his brightness by a few million watts.

My brain was definitely on overload. Even for a dream it was too much. Which may be why the brightness suddenly dimmed and I found myself looking directly into the theater manager's flashlight. I didn't hear everything he said, but it was pretty easy to tell he wasn't too happy, so I got up and left.

That was a couple hours ago. Now, back at our

camp, I carefully set down what was left of Nelson's burned up phone book and rose to my feet. Dawn was just about to break. I could already hear the sun tuning up. And as I stood there, all by myself, it hit me again how lonely I was. I don't want to complain, I know it was my own fault, but to be honest, I'd never felt so alone. Or stupid. I mean everyone else was smart enough to go along with the crowd, so what was wrong with me?

That's when I heard it. It was real soft, like the wind blowing, but there was no mistaking Trashman's song. I looked all around but of course nobody was there. Well, nobody except Saffron. I spotted her down at the bottom of the slope, making her way up. She was wearing her royal robe again, the one with those diamonds and emeralds which, of course, I would never mention.

"She motioned to what was left of the camp and shouted, "What the (*insert expletive*) happened?

"They found us." I called back.

She shook her head and continued climbing. I noticed she was carrying a big book under her arm. She stopped a moment to check out the burned Christmas bush then kept coming. When she finally arrived, she took a moment to catch her breath and do some more cussing. Then she turned and looked out over the city with me. In the growing light we could see gray tendrils of smoke rising from the buildings over in the financial district.

"(*Expletive*)," she said.

I nodded.

"(*Expletive, expletive*)."

I nodded again. When she's right, she's right.

Then she frowned. "You hear that?"

I shrugged. "I hear lots of things."

"No, that noise. Like a flute or something."

"Oh that," I said. "It's just something leftover from my dream."

She gave me one of those looks then turned back to the city. "So where'd everybody go?"

"They're in town helping the O.R.B."

"But not you? You didn't go with them."

I shrugged again. "I can't."

We heard more firecrackers going off in the distance.

"It's gonna be bad," she said.

I nodded and looked down at her book. Now I could see it was the Reverend's Ancient Text. "Did the Reverend give that to you?" I asked.

"Yeah . . . he just don't know it, yet." She caught me staring at it. "You know how to read?"

"Sure."

"Good." She shoved it at me. "Merry Christmas."

"Christmas is not for another—"

"It's a figure of speech, moron."

"Oh, right." I chuckled like we both knew it was a joke.

But as soon as I touched it, I felt it moving. Not really moving. More like vibrating. And in perfect time to the music. "Wow," I said.

"Wow what?"

"You know, the book. It's vibrating. With the music."

She gave me another one of those looks. "Don't start up that (*insert another expletive*) with me, you (*expletive*).

I nodded, deciding not to press my luck. Instead, I just closed my eyes, wrapped both arms around the book and held it to my chest. As I did, I felt the music vibrating into me . . . just like my dreams.

"What are you grinning about, Dough Face?"

"I'm sorry," I said. But no matter how hard I tried, I couldn't make myself look sad. And the longer I held the book, the more the music soaked in.

"You really are an idiot, aren't you?"

I nodded and grinned.

She shook her head and swore. "In case you haven't noticed, things ain't exactly in a happy state right now."

I nodded again but I barely heard. Because the music had turned into words. Not with lyrics or anything like that. They were still notes, but they were also words. Trashman's words. Not a lot. There were only eight or so, but they went on forever. Not that they were drawn out to go slow and they never repeated themselves, but somehow, they went on and on . . . always fresh, always new. And always the same:

"Now you are ready," they said. *"Now you will rule."*

I looked back out over the city.

"Now you are ready. Now you will rule."

I still didn't understand what they meant, but as they kept soaking in, I knew one thing. If Trashman said them, they were true. I may not be the brightest crayon on the birthday cake, but as far back as I can remember, he had never lied. So I guess I didn't have to understand.

"Now you are ready. Now you will rule."

Because if he said them, I was just fool enough to believe them.

ENDNOTES

Chapter Three

[1]The King James Bible, 2 Corinthians 5:17

[2]The New King James Bible, 2 Peter 1:4

Chapter Eight

[3]The NIV Bible, Romans 8:28

[4]Ibid. Romans 12:2

[5]Ibid. James 1:2-4

Chapter Eleven

[6]Ibid. Ezekiel 22:29

[7]The King James Bible, James 4:4

[8]Ibid. James 4:8

[9]Ibid. Psalm 7:11

[10]Ibid. Matthew 5:48

Chapter Fourteen

[11]Ibid. Nahum 1:2

[12]The NIV Bible, Malachi 3:2

[13]The King James Bible, 2 Kings 2:13

[14]The NIV Bible, 2 Corinthians 3:6

[15]The King James Bible, Romans 6:23

Chapter Fifteen

[16]The NIV Bible, Deuteronomy 31:6 (paraphrased)

[17]The King James Bible, Rev 6:17

[18]The King James Bible, Exodus 22:23

Chapter Eighteen

[19]Benjamin Franklin

[20]The King James Bible, James 2:20

[21]Ibid. James 2:7

[22]The NIV Bible, Joshua 11:12

[23]The King James Bible, Deuteronomy 7:2

[24]Ibid. Isaiah 2:12

[25]Ibid. Proverbs 3:34

[26]Ibid. Luke 6:26

[27]The NIV Bible, Jude 1:16

[28]The King James Bible, Job 25:6

[29]Ibid. Isaiah 64:6

[30]Ibid. Job 21:30

[31]Ibid. Isaiah 59:18

[32]The NIV Bible, Matthew 13:42

Chapter Nineteen

[33]The NIV Bible, Ephesians 2:6

[34]Ibid. 1 Corinthians 6:2-3

[35]Ibid. Romans 8:17

[36]Ibid. John 17:22

[37]King James Bible, Genesis 3:5

[38]Ibid. Isaiah 42:8

[39]Ibid. Deuteronomy 6:4

[40]Ibid. Isaiah. 44:6

[41]Ibid. Deuteronomy32: 39

[42]Ibid. Deuteronomy 4:39

[43]Ibid. 2 Kings 19:15

[44]Ibid. Exodus 20:3

[45]Ibid. Psalm 97:9

[46]Ibid. Matthew 12:30

Chapter Twenty-seven

[47] Probably some old Greek or Mafia guy.

Soli Deo gloria

OTHER BOOKS BY BILL MYERS

NOVELS

The Judas Gospel
The God Hater
The Voice
Angel of Wrath
The Wager
Soul Tracker
The Presence
The Seeing
The Face of God
When the Last Leaf Falls
ELI
Blood of Heaven
Threshold
Fire of Heaven

CHILDREN BOOKS

Baseball for Breakfast (picture book
The Bug Parables (picture book series)
Imager Chronicles (fantasy series)
McGee and Me (book/video series)
The Incredible Worlds of Wally McDoogle (comedy series)
Blood Hounds, Inc. (mystery series)
The Elijah Project (suspense series)
Secret Agent Dingledorf and his trusty dog, Splat (comedy
series)
TJ and the Time Stumblers (comedy series)
Truth Seekers (action/comedy series)

TEEN BOOKS

Faith Encounter (devotional)
*Hot Topics, Tough Question*s (non-fiction)
Forbidden Doors (supernatural series)

Dark Power Collection
Invisible Terror Collection
Deadly Loyalty Collection
Ancient Forces Collection
The Dark Side of the Supernatural (non-fiction)

E-BOOK SERIES
Supernatural Love
Supernatural War"

For a further list of Bill's books, sample chapters, and reviews go to www.Billmyers.com You can also go there to sign up for his newsletter announcing future releases. Or check out his Facebook page
www.facebook.com/billmyersauthor

© Copyright 2015 Bill Myers

52729987R00115

Made in the USA
Charleston, SC
24 February 2016